The phone rang six times before it was answered.

"This is Elizabeth Trenka, calling about your notice in the supermarket."

A gruff male voice said, "Which notice? The typing?"

"Yes," Betty said.

"Got references? Ever been in jail? Honest and trustworthy?"

"If necessary, to the first question. No, to the second. And as to the third, I'm applying to type, not to handle your money. I have worked extensively in offices. I don't drink, I don't take drugs, and I have a sufficient number of possessions that I don't need to steal more from you."

"Not a struggling young writer, are you?"

"Definitely not."

"You sound insubor⸺

"I speak my mind,'

DEATH AT FACE VALUE

Joyce Christmas

FAWCETT GOLD MEDAL • NEW YORK

A Fawcett Gold Medal Book
Published by Ballantine Books
Copyright © 1995 by Joyce Christmas

Library of Congress Catalog Card number: 94-96485

ISBN 0-449-14801-7

Manufactured in the United States of America

First Edition: April 1995

10 9 8 7 6 5 4

For Ed Pemberton and Bob Coyne

Grow old with me
Better dial tone is yet to be . . .

CHAPTER 1

"THIS IS your life, Elizabeth Anne Trenka . . ."

The words from that old, old TV show flitted through Betty Trenka's mind as she signaled a left turn into the parking lot of the East Moulton, Connecticut, supermarket.

It is my life, she thought, and that's a fact, much as I have been trying to resist it.

The lot was fairly full even early on a weekday morning, but she found a spot close to the entrance. That meant she could duck in and out without too much outdoor conversation with her fellow townsfolk on a chilly late-fall day. The strategies of small-town living were coming back to her.

Indeed, in the couple of months she'd been living there since her move from a suburb of Hartford, she felt herself falling back easily into the small-town life she'd left behind more than forty years before.

She got out of her nearly new Buick and felt in the pocket of her dark-green loden coat for her shopping list.

"Damn," she said aloud. She'd left it behind on the kitchen counter. Forgetfulness bothered her. She didn't believe that at sixty-three she'd lost her sharpness—even though Sid Edwards Junior had effectively forced her to retire from Edwards & Son "because of her age." Well, he'd done the same to his own father, and no one was sharper than Sid Edwards Senior.

"Oooh-hooo, Betty!"

Betty looked around and saw Molly Perkins, who ran the town drugstore with her husband, the pharmacist, advancing on her with a shopping cart loaded with overflowing brown

1

bags. She was red-cheeked, middle-aged, and incurably nosy.

"Morning, Molly," Betty said. She'd hoped that living in a new place and introducing herself right off as Elizabeth would mean no one would ever call her Betty again. It hadn't worked, with the exception of her neighbor on Timberhill Road, Edward Kelso.

"A real bite in the air," Molly said. "Winter's on the way for sure. Say, Miz Fuller tells me you've started volunteering at the library. You'll get to meet a lot of really *nice* folks doing that. Just what you need."

Molly was hinting once again that a single, retired past-middle-age lady must surely be lonely, living on a sparsely populated country road a mile from town. Taller than average, not a helpless old thing, and odd-looking, too, what with her thick glasses and her heavy hair pinned up in back, those long skirts and sensible shoes. Molly was convinced that Betty must need to make friends like crazy.

Wrong, to a degree. Betty had never needed a lot of people outside her office life, only a congenial few.

But also true, in a sense. Her reluctant retirement hadn't yet taken an acceptable shape of comfortable routines and modest pleasures. Raking autumn leaves and worrying about the state of the furnace as winter approached lacked the satisfactions of being office manager par excellence and keeping Edwards & Son running smoothly. She needed something more to fill the days and years ahead. Well, she was beginning to make the effort.

"I'm enjoying the library very much" was all that Betty said about her one-morning-a-week volunteering. The librarian was distinctly dictatorial, which didn't sit well with Betty, who was accustomed to being in charge. And the high-school girls who had somehow been coerced into volunteering seemed unanimously bored with the whole idea of books. On the other hand, the adults who loved reading were pleasant, and the children who hadn't been so spoiled by television to make the concept of books unfamiliar were actually delightful.

"That's what I mean. *Nice* people." Molly's eyes flickered toward the supermarket. "You have to be so careful . . ." Betty knew what she was getting at. News got around fast.

"I'm also finding it pleasant to help Carole learn to type," Betty said sweetly. She hadn't been in East Moulton long enough to know every reason that people disapproved of Carole, the regular morning checkout person at the supermarket, but she had a good idea. Carole was young, with a mass of frizzed hair in the popular uncombed celebrity style. She was certainly pretty, but the hint of a voluptuous body beneath her blue smock, the lush, pouty lips, and the dark-fringed, seductive eyes were perhaps more than a small Connecticut town could handle. That, and the fact that she was an outsider who had arrived in East Moulton under less than auspicious circumstances some months before as the purported wife of a legendary town troublemaker. Johnny Fender had been away for several years, but on his return he had promptly abandoned Carole and the little girl she had in tow. Hers, his, or theirs, Betty didn't know. Carole hadn't confided in her, although she'd seen the adorable five-year-old once. In any case, being Johnny Fender's consort hadn't enhanced Carole's reputation.

Penny Saks, Betty's neighbor on Timberhill Road, had filled her in on all that early in the game.

"Johnny Fender was real cute," Penny had told Betty. "The girls in high school were crazy about him, but he was the worst kid in town. That awful mother of his sure has something to be proud of." Penny, a cheerful young mother of three blond boys and devoted to her husband, Greg, adored a good, gossipy, dramatic tale. "He could talk a rock into committing a felony. Johnny left town first because of trouble with the police, they say. Whitey had just turned two."

Since all three Saks boys were called Whitey, that hadn't meant much to Betty.

"He came back last spring," Penny had said, "with Carole and little Noelle. Johnny's mother was furious. No room in East Moulton for two Mrs. Fenders—if they really *were* married. Then Johnny disappeared again, and left Carole to get along for herself." Penny added uncharitably, "She's not like us. I can't imagine why she stayed on here. She'd be better off somewhere else."

It hadn't been difficult to start teaching Carole the rudiments of typing so she could one day get an office job. Betty had, after all, once spent some weeks teaching typing to Sid Junior's niece to whom he had given a summer clerical job that she was in no way capable of filling. In fact, on this morning's trip to the supermarket, Betty planned to fix a time for the next lesson when little Noelle could be with a neighbor.

"I was thinking, Betty"—Molly Perkins started to transfer bags of groceries to the backseat of her car parked two spaces from Betty's spot—"you need company. Frank Travis's retriever just had a litter of the cutest puppies you ever saw. . . ."

"I expect to be doing some traveling soon," Betty said hastily. At least she was reading up on places she'd always dreamed of visiting and now could, thanks to the money Sid Edwards Senior had seen she'd gotten. "I couldn't take the responsibility."

"They're sooo adorable. . . ."

Betty shook her head. In all her sixty-three years, Betty had never been an animal person.

"There's that spare room at your place," Molly said as she got into her car. "You could take in a boarder."

"Perhaps," Betty said. She had also never been a roommate person. It was a relief to hear the engine of Molly's car start. She was beginning to get cold standing out in the parking lot.

Molly rolled down her window. "You have to come to dinner with Perk and me some night soon," she said. "Maybe you can persuade Mr. Kelso to come along. I've never had any luck getting him over to our place. I've told him a hundred times it wouldn't be a problem, but I can't convince him."

Betty only smiled politely. Her neighbor Ted Kelso was a fanatic and indeed a magnificent cook. Betty was certain he was disinclined to partake of Molly's tuna casserole following an undistinguished glass of sherry and some corn chips and sour cream dip. The fact that he was largely confined to a wheelchair would be his perfect excuse for turning down Molly—although he never felt hampered about going anyplace he really wanted to go.

Molly eased out of her parking space and offered the inevitable parting shot. "You think about those puppies," she said. "Purebred. And I've been meaning to ask you. Is some place for sale out your way? Somebody was asking about Timberhill Road just the other day."

"Not that I know of," Betty said.

"Probably someone looking for that character who fixed up the old Winfield farm."

Betty waved to the departing Molly and trudged through the brisk autumn day toward the supermarket entrance. The mall out on the highway had a vast supermarket, and shops with everything one could possibly want, but Betty's needs were simple enough that the local stores were sufficient.

"Hiya, Miz Trenka." Carole lowered the supermarket tabloid she'd been reading and waved from her cash register. Betty waved back. The headlines on the paper said something about a Tragic Love Triangle in Tinseltown. The outside world impinged relentlessly on little backwaters like East Moulton, where the supermarket checkers donned vivid red lip gloss and darkened their lashes with advanced-formula mascara, the better to total up the processed cheese, sugar-coated cereal, and frozen pizzas for the townsfolk.

Not for the first time Betty reminded herself that young people were different nowadays, but Carole really was in need of some adult guidance.

Betty pushed her shopping cart past the produce department displays and picked out some bananas and a couple of Granny Smith apples. She got orange juice and six-grain

bread produced by a local bakery. Ted Kelso had urged her
to try it, and she'd come to love it.

Two or three people murmured greetings as they passed
her in the aisles. People were getting to know her from seeing her along Main Street and at the library.

Betty had been planning to try out a recipe for pasta
sauce she'd found in a magazine, but with her list left behind, she couldn't be sure she'd remember all the ingredi-
ents.

Now that she had more leisure than she knew how to fill,
she was turning away from quick frozen dinners, sand-
wiches, and salads, and even her old tried-and-true company chicken dishes.

She gave up trying to remember what was on the list and
bought a couple of lean pork chops, frozen green beans,
and a baking potato.

"Sorry," she said quickly as she absentmindedly brushed
shopping carts with a young woman with a stupendous pile
of groceries: great slabs of steak in clear wrap, liters and liters of soft drinks, stacks of frozen vegetables, and many
large bags of taco and potato chips.

"No problem," the woman said as Betty moved on.
"Have a nice day." Betty observed briefly the huge con-
cealing sunglasses, the floppy brimmed hat, and the shiny
knee-high leather boots over the tightest imaginable jeans.
Small-town housewives were certainly a different breed
nowadays: expensive but casual high fashion for a trip to
the supermarket. What were things coming to?

Then she had to smile to herself. She sounded like one
of the town's mildly censorious gossips.

"I hear you've got a boyfriend from out of town," Carole
said coyly as Betty unloaded her cart at the register. Apparently some townspeople condescended to share the latest
news with Carole.

"A very old friend came to visit," Betty said. When she
was living near Hartford, she and Eugene Salzman had met
faithfully for bimonthly Sunday brunches, but it had taken
Eugene a long time to finally make his way from Spring-

field to East Moulton. The fact that he'd stayed overnight had probably set everyone agog, but never mind. Let the town revel in speculation about its most recent senior citizen. In any case, strictly platonic was perhaps an understatement where Eugene was concerned.

At the same time, the town also enjoyed its quiet speculations about Betty's friendship with Ted Kelso, which had come about because both had been briefly at the center of a situation involving murder. It would do no good to point out that Ted was a good twenty years Betty's junior.

"So what did Mr. Kelso have to say about your visitor?" Carole asked as she rang up Betty's items. "Jealous?"

Betty laughed. "Not likely. Mr. Kelso is still up in Boston on business, so I didn't have a chance to introduce them on this visit."

"Amazing, don't you think? The way Mr. Kelso manages?"

"Ted? I don't believe he thinks of it as 'managing,' " Betty said. "I think he considers it 'living.' "

Carole looked puzzled, then said, "I guess you're right." She nodded. "Yeah, that's right. Living." Suddenly the cheery smile vanished, and Carole blinked. Betty hoped she wasn't about to become weepy. That was one thing Betty didn't miss at all about life at Edwards & Son—dealing with the girls' personal problems that accompanied them to the office and required counseling in order to keep the business on track.

In spite of not really wanting to know, Betty said, "Is something wrong, Carole?"

"No!" she said quickly. "I'm just tired. Taking care of Noelle and working here and living in that lousy house on the wrong side of town and never having any fun. I hate this place."

Betty did know that there were better ways for a young woman to live than in the midst of a hostile town. She wondered briefly, as Penny Saks had, why she simply didn't leave. Possibly she was hoping that the typing lessons would give her a marketable skill in some distant city.

"We'll soon have you typing like a demon," Betty said, "and then I'll show you all about the computer . . ."

Suddenly Carole wouldn't look at Betty as she bagged the groceries. She took a deep breath. "I might not need more lessons," she said. "I mean, like, something might turn up that could mean good money."

Betty opened her mouth to ask what she meant, then quickly decided not to. Carole was pointedly absorbed in counting out her change. Then another customer arrived at the checkout counter, and Carole turned away from Betty. "You have a nice day now, Miz Trenka," she murmured over her shoulder.

The customer, a solid, gray-haired matron who was a regular library borrower and favored sexy romance novels, nodded to Betty and ignored Carole. No wonder the poor girl hated East Moulton.

On her way out of the supermarket, Betty stopped at the community bulletin board. Her notice about an experienced office worker being available for temporary employment was still pinned up. However, it had brought her only one disastrous office-temp job and then two at-home jobs typing a résumé and a handful of indignant Letters to the Editor from a town resident who was incensed by a tax measure being debated by the state legislature. Betty had fixed up the sentences a bit so they flowed nicely, even if the argument was largely incomprehensible.

In the hope that opportunities would begin to come thick and fast, she'd supplemented her old portable with an inexpensive computer and printer.

The sign about Frank Travis's golden retriever puppies was there, complete with a Polaroid, but notices about boys willing to mow lawns had faded with the summer. She was starting to recognize the names of the seamstresses, the people with a piano for sale, the baby-sitters. She now knew the locations of the church bake sales and the volunteer fire department's ladies' auxiliary potluck suppers.

Thumbtacked high on the board she saw a new notice.

Since she was nearly six feet tall, she could easily read the elegant italic handwriting on a thick, creamy card:

I wish to engage an excellent typist to work at home on confidental material. I will pay well for the right person.

There was just a telephone number, no name. Betty copied down the number and waited until Carole was free of her current customer, who happened to be the behatted, booted young woman Betty had bumped into. When the woman had pushed her overflowing cart away from the register toward the door, Betty said, "Do you know who posted that new typing notice, Carole?"

Carole seemed not to have heard. She was gazing enviously after the young woman, who had just spent ninety-seven dollars on groceries. The young woman seemed to sense Carole's stare. She turned back at the exit and looked at Carole with a half-smile. Carole's envy of the young woman's glamour and affluence was obvious.

"The notice . . ." Betty repeated.

Carole looked wary. "I wasn't here when it was put up. Funny they didn't think to call you, with your notice staring right at them. But isn't that the way? You see these personal ads from a guy who likes walks in the woods who's looking for a five-foot blonde in her twenties, and right next to it, the five-foot blonde he's dreaming about wants a guy to take long walks with. They probably never call each other." Carole looked glum, perhaps wondering if there was a guy out there for her to take long walks with through the woods. Then she said softly, "I really appreciate what you did for me, Miz Trenka. Noelle and me will be okay."

"Good," Betty said, but she was thinking, I hope so. However, if she'd learned one thing in all those years at Edwards & Son, it was never to force more confidences from her girls than they were willing to offer.

Betty shoved her modest bag of purchases onto the backseat. The blue-jeaned woman with the hat and sunglasses was depositing her many bags in the trunk of an elegant maroon car. Betty thought it was a Mercedes. A very high-toned vehicle for East Moulton.

Betty pulled into the driveway beside her cozy little house, new to her but many decades old, and dumped her groceries in the kitchen. The missing shopping list was right there on the counter. Her next act was to call the number from the bulletin board.

The phone rang six times before it was answered.

"This is Elizabeth Trenka, calling about your notice in the supermarket."

A gruff male voice said, "Which notice? The typing?"

"Yes," Betty said.

"Got references? Ever been in jail? Honest and trustworthy?"

"If necessary, to the first question. No, to the second. And as to the third, I'm applying to type, not to handle your money. I have worked extensively in offices. I don't drink, I don't take drugs, and I have a sufficient number of possessions that I don't need to steal more from you."

"Not a struggling young writer, are you?"

"Definitely not."

"You sound insubordinate."

"I speak my mind," Betty said.

"I'll try you out. Can you be here tonight about seven for an interview? The old Winfield farm. Know where that is?"

"I'll find it." It was, she knew, a mile or so past her house.

"Afraid of dogs?"

"Only if they're openly hostile," she said.

"Ha. Good answer. Ever lived in New York?"

"No. Just occasional visits."

"That's what I like, simple, small-town women who scorn the bright lights and dark lusts of the city. Nothing but trouble there, take it from a man who knows the worst." He sounded positively delighted to be that man. "What did you say your name was?"

Betty told him again, emphasizing the "Elizabeth."

"Seven. Be on time." The man hung up, not having bothered to give his name.

A simple, small-town woman was she? Betty was amused. The interview was likely to be entertaining.

I'll go to the Winfield farm, Betty thought, but I may have advanced beyond employment by rude, demanding men.

Then she thought it was quite remarkable what retired ladies will do to keep up the semblance of being useful and productive without going to the trouble of acquiring a pet or a roommate.

CHAPTER 2

THE SMELL of death seeped out from under the closed door of the bedroom and crept into the corners of the small Manhattan apartment.

The fat black-and-white cat that sat on the windowsill didn't notice the smell. It was studying the iron slats of the fire escape beyond the curtain that stirred now and then as a breath of chilly wind blew in through the open window.

Death, in any case, was not a concern of the cat's. It had never ventured outside the apartment into the New York City jungle, and thus had never killed a bird or a field mouse for its own or its mistress's pleasure.

The cat put a tentative paw outside the window. The screen and the flimsy iron gate that were always in place were missing. The intriguing possibility of a break for freedom onto the fire escape stirred briefly in the cat's mind.

Frankly, the cat was bored, and somewhat displeased at being left alone. It did not deal in time frames per se, but it seemed a long time since it had seen the woman who regularly filled the food bowl, often with treats like a handful of pink shrimp or a tasty bite of liver, who stroked its fur and babbled noisily all the time. The other one, the one behind the closed bedroom door, hadn't made a sound for a long time, but the cat seldom paid her any attention. She was a stranger who was not kind to the cat, one of several girls who stayed for a time and moved on.

At least one food bowl was still half filled with dry food. Only the faint fishy odor of the last shrimp clung to the other bowl.

The cat had certainly already forgotten the loud person noises that had earlier driven it to hide behind the over-stuffed armchair in the living room. In any case, "earlier" could have been an hour before, a day, two days.

The phone in the living room started to ring again. It rang several times, but the cat ignored it. The phone rang often in the apartment. If neither woman answered, then the answering machine came on with an impersonal man's voice giving the number and asking for a brief message after the tone.

Now, at the sound of the tone, a woman said, "Mandi, it's Alison again. I know it's early, but you've gotta call Rosie *right away. Now.* She's not mad at you. You're still with the agency, okay? Viola, if you're back in town, *please* call Rosie and tell her what's going on with Mandi. This is, like, you know, a disaster. She's missed three days of bookings."

The cat liked hearing the sound of a human voice.

It was quiet again. The cat licked a paw and passed it thoughtfully behind its ear. The sky was a pale blue now. As the autumn sun began to rise on Manhattan, blinds were raised in the tall modern apartment building across the back alley from the five-story walkup with the fire escape, where the cat lived on the second floor.

A dead geranium in a terra-cotta pot out on the fire escape looked promising. The cat leaned out and tested the slats with a paw, then withdrew quickly.

The sound of footsteps came from outside in the hallway. The cat heard them often enough as tenants on the upper floors passed by, but this time they were many and heavy. Then there were voices.

At the first heavy knock on the door, the cat moved with surprising quickness, considering its size. In a moment it was safely behind the armchair as the knocks became pounding and a man's rough voice said, "Open up. Police. Anybody home?"

"I haven't seen either of them for days," a woman's voice said, "but I go out early, so I don't run into them much. The girl's modeling agency says nobody answers the phone, so they got my number and asked me to look. I couldn't, not alone. I do hope Mrs. Roman's all right."

The lock thumped as the key was turned. The cat peered out cautiously from behind the chair, perhaps in the hope that it was someone with shrimp in hand.

The door swung open and there were people in the doorway.

One of the big men coughed. "Oh, jeez. Get back, lady. There's something dead in here."

"Mrs. Roman has a cat," the woman said nervously, and peered in between the two men in the doorway. "She does love that cat."

"No dead cat smells like that," the other man said. They took one step into the apartment.

The woman hung back. "I hope nothing's happened. Mrs. Roman's not so young. Viola Roman, a lovely woman. She keeps herself just so."

The men stood just inside the door, hands behind their backs, touching nothing.

"And that pretty little girl who stays with her," the woman went on. "Oh, God, what if something terrible has happened to her? No one's safe in this city anymore."

She stopped when the two uniformed policemen looked at her.

"That room, what is it?" one of the men asked, and pointed to the closed door.

"The bedroom," the woman said from the doorway. "This is a one-bedroom. The girls who stay when they come to New York to work, they use the bedroom, Mrs. R. told me. She sleeps on the daybed."

"What about these girls?"

"Models, actresses from out of town. They stay a few weeks until they find a place of their own. Maybe they pay Mrs. Roman a bit against the rent, but they're no trouble. I don't ask questions."

"The police ask the questions," the other man said. "You wait out there in the hall, while we find out what's what."

"I *am* responsible," the woman said hesitantly. She was torn between wanting to know everything and not wanting to know the worst.

"Not for this, I hope," the policeman said.

The woman backed out into the hall. "I'll stay right here. Mind the cat. It's touchy." She hovered as the policemen advanced carefully into the room.

"What do you think, Norm?" one of the men said. "Break-in? Window's open."

"Nothing's messed up, Eddie, and the door was locked. Look at this place." He surveyed the walls covered with framed photos, the knickknacks on every flat surface, as though the occupant's every memory had been retained in some useless object. "I mean, you'd know if somebody had ransacked the place. But I hate to think what's in the bedroom. Ah!" He caught sight of the cat which had ventured, plump and stately, from behind the chair. "Take the cat out of here, give it to the dame in the hall," Norm said.

"Not me, Norm. I don't like cats. I'd rather take a look at what's in the bedroom." Eddie eyed the cat, which stared at him unblinkingly.

"The girl's name is Mandi," the woman said from the hall. "Real pretty. A model, Mrs. R. said."

The cat continued to examine the people, none of whom made a move that indicated food was imminent.

The policeman called Eddie walked carefully toward the closed door. It swung open with a nudge from his toe. He peered in and jerked back.

"Norm, you gotta go downstairs to the car and call the supervisor at the precinct," he said. "This one's good and dead. Tell them to send the homicide cops right away. And get that cat out of here. It's not going to hurt you."

But it did.

The cat didn't like being picked up by a stranger, especially one who stepped on its tail with a uniformed policeman's large shoe. He looked at the bloody scratch on his hand.

"I told you it was touchy," the woman said smugly.

"Give it here." The lump of cat reluctantly assumed a place in the manager's arms. "Tina is Mrs. Roman's precious," she said. "I can't abide cats myself."

"Yeah, well. Why don't you wait downstairs? Try to remember if you noticed any gentlemen callers for the girl or heard any funny noises the past couple of days," Eddie said. "The plainclothes guys will want to know everything you can tell them."

"I never notice anything," the woman said. "Not with the television on." As she departed downward, she said over her shoulder, "Mrs. Roman didn't allow the girls to have boyfriends coming up here, but that's not to say what they did when she was away. I've seen cars picking Mandi up on the street. Now and then I've seen men coming to call, but," she added hastily, "I wouldn't recognize them." Then she and the cat were out of sight at the bottom of the stairs.

"What a city," Norm said. He was planning on seeing a doctor about the scratch on his hand as soon as he could. "What a life. My two girls wouldn't be getting picked up by cars in front of the house, I can tell you that. The wife wants to move to the suburbs. Hell, she wants to live in the country. Trees and grass. No dead bodies. Maybe she's right."

Eddie watched Norm examine the scratch. He said, "I hope the homicide guys get here fast. I want an early lunch." Then he gazed at the living room, where they'd been careful to touch nothing. "It's got to have been somebody she knew."

"The woman who lives here?" Norm was wondering if there was iodine in the bathroom for his scratch, but he'd catch hell if he disturbed anything in the apartment.

Eddie shook his head. "You never know, but the girl was lying there in the bedroom in that pink nightie, looking . . ." He shook his head. "Young kids from the sticks get eaten alive by this city. You see it all the time."

"It's not our problem, Eddie," Norm said. "Let's call the precinct."

CHAPTER 3

THE MAILMAN had left a meager pile of mail in Betty's mailbox: two bills, two catalogs for "current resident," one selling smoked meats, the other miniature shipbuilding materials. There was a scenic postcard from her old Hartford friend, Cora Welles, who was visiting her daughter in Los Angeles, and the monthly nonscenic postcard from her Cousin Rita in Boston. They kept in touch that way, neither of them saying much more than the weather is good/bad/atrocious; health is good/indifferent; keeping busy as usual; and from Rita always, "God bless you."

She was leafing through the mail, when a grimy blue car approached from the direction of the town center and slowed down as it passed her house as if searching the names on the mailboxes at the roadside. She watched it speed up and disappear around a curve. Betty tsked to herself. People tended to take that curve too fast. Even the locals found Timberhill Road a temptation for speeding, since traffic was usually light.

Betty carried her mail to the front door. As she entered the house, she glimpsed the same blue car returning, but this time it didn't slow at all as it passed. Somebody else lost on the meandering country roads around East Moulton.

She dropped her mail on the kitchen counter. She'd be writing her postcard to Rita next week, and Cora would probably call when she returned from California. Betty went out to her backyard. She really ought to be clearing out the single-car garage so she'd have a place to put her car when it snowed, but instead she opted to rake leaves.

17

The old padlock that didn't lock anymore held the two garage doors together, more or less. Betty tugged open the left-hand door. The white paint was peeling and the wood was dry. She'd have to get someone over to replace both doors before winter came.

The old garage smelled musty, and the small windows near the roof were so dusty, they let in only a glimmer of sunlight. The spiders seemed to like the place. There were clouds of webs in the corners that linked up with the clutter of boxes and broken-down lawn chairs in the middle of the space. She headed for the wall where a few rusty gardening tools hung, reached over an empty, old-fashioned trunk, avoided the handlebars of a decrepit bicycle, and grabbed the fairly respectable rake leaning against the wall.

She hadn't had much reason to enter the garage since she moved in, but in those few times she wondered about the people who had abandoned the clutter around her. Molly Perkins's uncle was one of them. He'd once owned the house, and a lot of the junk had probably belonged to his kids and grandkids, to judge by the box of dusty, broken toys. There had been some other residents who hadn't stayed long.

She stopped. The garage had a little back door that had always appeared to be nailed shut. Now it seemed to be slightly ajar. Betty picked her way through the rubbish she had to get rid of—and soon—and examined the door. It was shut, but it looked as though it had been recently opened. The spiderwebs hung in tatters and the knob looked clean—at least cleaner than anything else in the place.

The Saks boys from next door at it again, no doubt. All she needed was the trio of Whitey Sakses deciding to start a campfire in there. The volunteer fire department would never get to Timberhill Road in time to save the old building. On the other hand, that would save her the trouble of cleaning out the place.

She'd have to speak to Penny about the boys' possible

intrusion into the garage. They probably looked on the place as their private clubhouse.

Betty took her rake outside and began leisurely to rake up the yellow, red, and brown leaves into a big pile under the blue autumn sky.

A couple of cars passed the house, and she thought she glimpsed the maroon Mercedes she'd seen at the supermarket, although it was possible that Alida, her sprightly elderly neighbor on the other side, had decided to invest in a snappy new car in addition to climbing mountains and scuba diving. She was in her eighties, and constituted a sort of role model for Betty, who liked to think that at her neighbor's age she'd start thinking about learning to dive or sail or drive a race car.

Betty paused to take a deep breath. The air was crisp and full of the scent of dry leaves. A few of Ted Kelso's honeybees were making a last-minute tour of the remaining blooms in the scraggly garden Betty had inherited.

Today, retirement actually seemed quite pleasant. The anger at being sent packing from Edwards & Son had subsided over the past month or so.

After lunch Betty crossed the open field between her place and the Sakses' modern ranch-style house. Penny Saks was sure to know all about the Winfield farm, and given the town's taste for knowing everything about everything, she could probably also identify Betty's potential employer. Penny's car was in the driveway, and the smell of baking greeted Betty.

"Just in time for coffee and a couple of cookies," Penny said. She was perpetually perky, and kept busy from dawn till dusk.

Penny gathered up a piece of half-finished needlepoint from the kitchen table to make room for Betty. Penny was big on arts and crafts; indeed, the stenciling on about everything that didn't move, the wreathes of dried flowers, the needlework, the hand-made pottery mugs all attested to her determination to keep her hands busy even as the daytime soaps played on. Betty had so far resisted all of Penny's gentle efforts to involve her with needle, glue, or paint-brush.

"Somebody must have a house up for sale," Penny said. "Have you seen all the cars the past couple of days? It can't be Alida. She would have told me. Mr. Kelso isn't thinking of selling, is he? After all the work he's put into that place."

"I think Ted's well settled." Ted Kelso's low stone house across from Betty's had been entirely remodeled to provide easy access throughout for his wheelchair. "Penny, do you know the old Winfield farm?"

"That's not for sale anymore. And isn't it fabulous? A famous person living right in our town." Penny sounded thrilled. "He just settled in during the last week or so. He won't be here all year round. He spends time in New York, they say."

"Really? Who?" Betty was asking about both the alleg-edly famous person and "they," although she knew per-fectly well that "they" meant just about everyone in town. Molly had already taken note of the "character" at the farm.

Penny hesitated. "Someone mentioned his name, but I didn't recognize it. But he *is* famous. Everyone says so."

"How nice for East Moulton," Betty said. She didn't mention that the famous person was also somewhat rude.

"He bought the Winfield farm last spring and had it fixed up beautifully, they say. The renovation was handled by an out-of-town firm, so nobody really knows . . . Greg's thinking of going around to see if he needs insurance."

Good luck to Greg, Betty thought. "It's right nearby, isn't it? And haven't I seen the Winfield name around town?"

Penny nodded. "Winfield Street and Winfield Road. They're one of the founding families. All dead now. If you go along Timberhill Road away from here, there's an old road on your left. You can't miss it. There's a brand-new mailbox right on the corner. The farmhouse is way back in the woods. There used to be farm fields all around there and right over to the back of our property, yours, too, but nobody's farmed it for ages. Greg says somebody's sure to get the bright idea of building a development on that land." Her eyes brightened at the idea of many new prospects for Greg's insurance business. "The Winfield farmhouse is two hundred years old, at least." Penny shrugged. "Or maybe not so old. It's historic, but the town never could afford to buy it for, like, a tourist attraction."

"Washington slept there, I suppose?" Betty said.

Penny wrinkled her little nose. "I don't think Washington had any business around East Moulton. Ted Kelso would know about the history part. Nothing much ever happens around here, back then or now. Well, except for the murders of those poor women."

"That was a unique event, I'm sure," Betty said. She didn't care to bring up memories of her introduction to East Moulton, and she didn't want to confide her reasons for wanting to locate the Winfield farm.

Penny was suddenly alert and listening. "I don't like it when the boys are so quiet. That Whitey can get into more mischief . . ."

"Surely they're not home from school yet," Betty said.

Penny grinned sheepishly. "Silly me."

"By the way, Penny," Betty said carefully, "is there any chance the boys have been playing in my garage?"

"Why, no," Penny said, maybe too quickly. "Why would they do that?"

"Because it's there," Betty said. "Look, Penny, I'm not accusing the Whiteys of anything. I merely noticed that it looked as though someone had been in there."

Penny sighed. "They do play in the woods out back, but they've been told not to go into any buildings. Of course, your place was empty for a couple of years, and boys being what they are . . . I'll lay down the law when they get home from school." She slapped her forehead suddenly. "School! I almost forgot. Did you hear the latest?" Penny leaned forward over the kitchen table and almost whispered, "They're saying somebody is selling drugs right next to the high school. They were talking about it at the PTA meeting. Can you imagine it?"

Betty could. She read not only the local papers, which tended to report births, deaths, and marriages, club activities and school events, but also *The Hartford Courant* and *The New York Times*, and watched the network television news programs, the better to keep up with the rapid decline of civilization.

"Yes," she said, "I can imagine it very easily. Times and people are different from when I was young. Probably even different from when you were in high school."

Penny laughed. "That was an *age* ago." Penny was perhaps in her early thirties. When had fifteen or so years become an "age"? To Betty, it was yesterday.

"Anyhow, that PTA meeting was full of news," Penny went on. "They were talking about your friend from the supermarket—"

"What about Carole?" Betty asked warily. "She seems like a nice young woman, just lonely and unhappy."

Penny looked at Betty as though she were a half-blind eternal optimist about people. "There are loads of rumors about *her*. They say she was seen at Al's Good Times, that tavern near the turnpike entrance. All got up and hanging out with a bunch of guys from out of town, drinking and dancing all night. Imagine leaving her little girl home alone. I don't blame her for wanting to have a good time, but the child . . . Beatrice Fender told somebody she was going to call the child welfare people."

"Now, Penny," Betty said somewhat sternly, "you're repeating rumors, which may not be all that they seem. You don't know Carole was actually at Al's, you don't know she left Noelle alone. She's told me a neighbor often looks after the child. And didn't you tell me yourself that Johnny Fender's mother hates Carole? Isn't it possible she's stirring up trouble?"

Penny looked momentarily ashamed. "Mrs. Fender isn't the most charitable person. She's actually a cousin of the last Winfields, or so Molly Perkins says. The black-sheep side." Penny got up to pour more coffee, and said hesitantly over her shoulder, "I have to tell you, Betty. People have been wondering why you're so interested in Carole, since she's so much younger."

Betty laughed. "A more-than-middle-aged single lady who's taken up with the pretty young thing at the supermarket? I gave her a couple of typing lessons, as everybody seems to know. I've spent my life trying to turn young women into functioning business people. Carole said she wanted a skill to help her get a better job. I wanted something to occupy my time while I got settled. It doesn't matter now. She seems to have found another job that doesn't require typing." Betty didn't care to think what that might be. "In a way she reminds me of a girl I knew years ago in my hometown. Anything to get out of town and find the good life." Betty sighed. "It's not always as good as it sounds. These cookies are delicious, Penny."

"And they're *so* easy to make," Penny said. "The boys are crazy about them. I'll give you the recipe. . . ." Betty had, at least, turned Penny away from idle gossip about poor Carole.

Betty carried the recipe across the field and entered her house in time to hear the ring of her telephone. Evidently it was the last ring, because she heard only the dial tone when she picked up the receiver.

She put away the recipe in a drawer in her kitchen. She wasn't yet prepared to whip up a batch of boy-attracting treats. Later, after the school bus had released the Saks boys, she heard them whooping and shouting across the field between the two houses.

Late in the afternoon, as she was examining her closet full of now-unused business clothes to decide what to wear to her interview at the Winfield farm, Betty caught sight of Ted Kelso's car pulling into his drive across the street. He was back from Boston earlier than expected. The car disappeared behind the house, where the convenient ramp allowed Ted to get from car to wheelchair to house.

Once more the phone started ringing, and this time she picked up quickly. She heard a soft voice, unidentifiable as to gender.

"Elizabeth Trenka?"

"Yes. Who is speaking?"

The line disconnected.

Betty stared at the phone. Her prospective employer checking up on her? Someone who'd seen her ad in the supermarket and gotten cold feet? More likely. A young-sounding voice though. She hesitated. Although she wasn't yet in the telephone book, her number could be found through the information operator. She was tempted to call Ted Kelso to learn the name of the new owner of the Winfield farm. He might be a well-known eccentric with a taste for making mysterious phone calls.

Still she hesitated. She and Ted Kelso enjoyed a few pleasant dinners and some interesting conversations, but he remained a mostly distant and rather private person. She didn't want to intrude unnecessarily on his homecoming activities.

Then she thought that she hadn't reached a position of responsibility at Edwards & Son by hesitating.

She dialed Ted's number.

"Yes?" Ted had a way of sounding wary when he answered the phone.

"It's Elizabeth," she said. Then it struck her that her mysterious caller had called her Elizabeth. "I know you just got home, but I need to know who now resides at the old Winfield farm."

Ted, not a spontaneously lighthearted soul, actually laughed. "A man named Crispin Abbott bought the place and fixed it up in grand style, they say. You must have heard of him."

"I might have heard the name."

"A real character," Ted said. "I met him a couple of times in New York years ago, when he was holding forth in his so-called literary and artistic salon down in Greenwich Village. I suppose it would be SoHo or TriBeCa nowadays. He fancies himself a genius. I'd say he's dabbled enough in the arts, enjoyed enough scandals, made enough enemies and friends in high places and married enough women to be notorious, but he's neither justly famous nor a genuine genius. In my opinion, naturally. Why do you ask?"

"He needs a typist," she said.

"Not you!"

"Well, perhaps. I'm seeing him this evening."

"Please, please come to dinner tomorrow and tell me about it. I'll be settled in by then. The Boston trip was pretty intense. And, Elizabeth, if you keep both your common sense and sense of humor about you, you'll probably enjoy an encounter with Crispin Abbott. He imagines himself a real lady-killer."

Not this lady, Betty thought.

Carole, released from her post at the cash register of the East Moulton Supermarket, sat in the driver's seat of her beat-up white Ford and looked at the heavy square card with the neat italic handwriting. Since she couldn't type, she hadn't bothered with the other card, but this one . . . This was something she could do. Someone wanted a muse, whatever that was. Someone to be a model. Good pay. She'd save the money to take her far, far away from this lousy place in case the promises that kept her here didn't work out. She'd learned not to rely too much on a guy's solemn promises.

She wasn't sure exactly what a "muse" did, but she figured she could fake that part. She'd certainly read all about models in the tabloids next to her register and in *People* and *Us* in the magazine rack at Molly Perkins's pharmacy. She'd looked at the fashion magazines, all those thin girls in their beautiful clothes who always looked as though they were gazing at themselves in a mirror and liking what they saw.

Models dated rock stars and married rich men who fulfilled their every wish. They had people to take care of their problems, nice cars to pick them up to go to the clubs and parties. They had closets full of clothes and tables of makeup and mirrors with lights around them. . . .

Carole jerked out of her reverie at the sound of someone pounding on the window next to her ear.

The angry face of Johnny's mother glared in. The flabby skin on Beatrice Fender's cheeks shook as she mouthed furious words that Carole couldn't hear through the glass. Carole started the engine and released the brake. That old witch wasn't going to make her late for the most important date of her life.

Mrs. Fender tottered back as the car moved ahead, and in the rearview mirror Carole could see her shaking a fist at the departing car. And just her luck. Three ladies who were regular customers at the supermarket were converging on the entrance from their cars and saw the whole thing.

Somebody's gonna say I tried to run her down, Carole thought. Not a bad idea, the old cow. Splat, right here in the parking lot.

That made her feel better. If things went okay, she'd be only a little late in picking up Noelle from the neighbor who looked after her between the time the school bus dropped her off from preschool and when Carole returned home from work.

"Hey, babe," she said aloud as she checked the mirror with one eye to be sure she looked all right, "it's going to be okay now."

Maybe she'd finally get out of this dumb town and make it to New York. She'd have a good life for Noelle, and she'd be able to forget some of the bad things she'd done to get this far.

Thanks to Johnny, she was a lot closer than she was a year ago. And no thanks to him that she might have found something good to carry her on to her dreams. She didn't need him to do the carrying.

The car behind her at the stoplight honked, and she saw that she'd been daydreaming while it turned green. The blue car passed her recklessly after they'd gone through the light, and Carole wrinkled her nose at the sight of the sloppy, plump man who was driving while wolfing down a fat sandwich.

She had to get out of this town as soon as she could manage it.

CHAPTER 4

THE TWO Manhattan homicide detectives who had come to Viola Roman's walkup on the heels of the discovery of Mandi Webb's body ended up spending many hours in the small, crowded apartment. The two uniformed men who had found the body had kept the crime scene untouched for the photographers and the medical people. Finally, the detectives, Danny Nealon and Fred Carver, watched the body of what had once been a very beautiful young woman being carried down the narrow stairs to the street in a body bag.

Danny and Fred looked again at the open window and the fire escape. They examined every inch of the small apartment cluttered with knickknacks, china figures of ballerinas, cunning ceramic kitties, vases of dried roses. They looked at the framed photos that covered the walls and at the closets stuffed with clothes neatly shrouded in plastic garment bags.

"Hatboxes," Dan had said on viewing a closet. "I haven't seen them since I was a kid." He was in his late forties, still alive after a long time on the force, and wondering if it was nearly time to retire. Fred was younger; he'd never seen a hatbox or anything like the wisps of net and velvet they contained. Danny remembered them from the old romantic black-and-white movies on TV that his wife liked to watch.

They had examined the extension cord that had been wrapped around the young woman's neck two or three days before, until her breathing had stopped, and she had been left dead on the floor of the narrow bedroom in a sexy pink peignoir.

They had examined the packets of letters and slips of paper with jotted names and addresses they'd taken from the tiny desk, all belonging to the official resident, Viola Roman. They had leafed through the dead girl's Filofax, and had found a schedule of recent modeling appointments never kept and a few men's names. Perhaps one of them was a violent, jealous boyfriend, former or current, who had gone out of control. They'd both seen that happen.

"Mandi Webb," Danny Nealon said. "Nineteen. Long-haired, long-legged blond. From South Dakota. I didn't know you could get to New York from there. She's been here maybe six months if I read the datebook right, signed on by his Rosellen modeling agency a few months ago. The agency says she hadn't kept her appointments or checked in for three days."

Fred Carver said, "Meanwhile, the woman who really rents the place is nowhere to be found."

The building manager had blanched when she identified the body as the girl who had been staying with Viola Roman for three or four weeks.

Fred said, "The manager says Roman 'used to be somebody,' whatever that means, and then she got old. You think she killed Mandi because she was young and beautiful? Maybe some man Roman liked preferred the younger one, so she got out the old extension cord . . ."

"You've been watching those soap operas again, Fred."

"Hey, stuff like that happens all the time."

Danny shrugged. "I don't see it, but this city makes people nuts. They all used to be someone once and got old or they're young and think they will be someone." He examined a huge framed black-and-white photograph on the wall: a sleek, elegant woman with a long, graceful neck and heavy, stylized makeup, gloves to the elbow, and posed in a dark full-skirted satiny ball gown, standing outdoors on sweeping stone steps. She was beautiful, aloof but sexy, sophisticated yet vulnerable. They'd actually laid down a huge carpet from the top of the steps to the bottom for her to stand on. The big church behind her, silhouetted against the night sky, looked familiar.

"Got it," Dan said aloud. "Roman. Viola Roman. That's Rome. The Spanish Steps. She really was somebody, Freddie, but I can't quite remember. It was a while ago."

There were many other framed photos on the walls, the same woman carefully posed and glamorous to an unreal degree. Photos from a distant decade, the fifties. The pictures stirred up memories of his oldest sister, thirty or thirty-five years ago, all dolled up for her high school prom in a green taffeta strapless formal gown. His father had hated Sis's boyfriend, and he'd hated that "indecent" dress, but she was a really nice dresser. You could hardly get into Sis's room with all the piles of fashion magazines. Every inch of the walls was covered with her favorite shots of glamorous models torn from their pages.

"What have they done to poor Mandi?"

A tall, slender woman paused in her rush through the doorway and threw back her head so that the long lines of her neck were not marred by any sagging skin. It was the woman in the photos, some decades older, but still beautiful.

"I've been out of town *all* week. I never *dreamed* anything like this would happen. I tried to guide her, protect her, I truly did. The poor child!"

"Mrs. Roman?" The two detectives looked her over.

In spite of her dramatic anguish, her eyes darted around the room, checking on her multitude of possessions. She was wearing a fashionable blue coat with a long darker blue scarf trailing after her. Unnaturally blond hair styled into a simple pageboy, careful makeup that successfully disguised the marks of age. Danny figured she must be close to sixty, but in this light, she managed to look fifteen years younger.

"Violetta," Danny said suddenly.

Viola Roman turned her head gracefully in his direction. "Of course," she said, suddenly composed at the sound of the name. She managed to place her feet and arms just so, and hold her head high, as though the camera were about to capture her. "They were after me, but they murdered Mandi by mistake."

"Ma'am, no one could have mistaken her for you." Fred Carver knew instantly that he'd not said the right thing.

The woman looked at him coldly.

"It was probably pretty dark," Danny said soothingly.

Viola Roman thawed a bit, and thereafter addressed her words solely to Danny. "Imagine if I'd been lying there asleep in the bedroom in the dark . . . I'd be dead now."

"Who would be after you?" The detective watched her with some interest. The legendary Violetta had certainly retained her allure. "And how would you know the girl had been found in the bedroom?"

The woman gestured gracefully with both hands. Her nails were beautifully manicured. "Mrs. Thing downstairs told me. The woman *can't* stop talking. I avoid her as much as possible. Wouldn't you? Naturally they'd creep up on her—me—when I was asleep. You know how they are. Ruthless and clever. How can one hide from them?"

The two detectives looked at each other. Perhaps the lady was a little unbalanced?

"Did this Mandi Webb have a boyfriend?" Danny decided not to pursue the matter of "them" for the present.

"Mandi had her admirers," Viola Roman said almost primly. "Men do find models irresistible. They always have. I can tell you that from personal experience, and it's much worse now with all the publicity about them. They're front-page news whatever they do. We didn't have that in my day. So these hopeful girls like Mandi come to New York stuffed with dreams of becoming the latest Naomi or Christie or Tyra or Jerry or Kate. . . . I can hardly keep their names straight. The new ones come to me for guidance because they know I understand the business. I do try to help them. I warn them that a career in this business lasts only a short time. You have to plan for the future. There are simply not enough millionaire rock stars to go around. They have to learn to keep a firm grip on reality."

The detectives exchanged glances. Viola Roman's grip on reality had not yet been established.

Danny said, "The reality here, ma'am, is that someone murdered Miss Webb in the past few days."

"I was away in New Jersey." She put her hand to her bosom. "Could I have stopped them if I had been here?"

Danny said, "It was likely someone she knew, since there was no break-in, and nothing was knocked over, no drawers pulled out. A boyfriend . . ."

"Her boyfriends did not visit here. It upsets Tina. My God, Tina! She must be terrified." Viola became agitated again and started to advance into the room. "Precious . . . come." She turned helplessly to the detectives. "My cat—" She stopped. "The window is open. I never leave it open. Someone was here after . . . after I left for New Jersey."

"The murderer," Danny said.

"Of course! How clever of you!" Again she started to edge into the apartment. Fred barred her way.

"Sorry, ma'am, we can't let you in just yet," he said. "We leave everything as it is for tonight, but we'll see that the place is secure when we leave."

"Ah, of course. Sorry. But I can't leave my cat."

"Your cat is downstairs with the manager."

Viola relaxed. Then she said tartly, "Tina *hates* that dreadful woman. With good reason, I might add." She turned abruptly and could be heard clattering down the stairs on very high heels.

"Roman probably knows the names of the dead girl's boyfriends," Fred said. "And if what you read in the papers is even half true, these models are really hot. Guys all over them."

"Freddie, you've been reading the *Post* and the *Daily News* and the *National Enquirer,* besides watching the soaps," Danny said with good humor. "Either the girl let someone in, or somebody had a key. Nobody came in through that window."

"The Roman woman has a key," Fred said, "even if she says she was away."

"We'll check on where she's been for the past few days."
Danny was gazing at the big photo of the young Violetta on
the Spanish Steps. "She's probably about my oldest sister's
age, but she still looks great."

"Aw, Danny. Don't go getting a crush on her," Fred said.
"She could be a murderer."

"People kill their intimates, not the paying guest," Danny
said. "There has to be a boyfriend somewhere. Let's go
downstairs."

The detectives found Viola in the manager's first-floor
apartment, cuddling the grotesquely plump black-and-white
cat.

"Tina and I will *not* stay in my apartment until you catch
the murderer," Viola Roman announced.

"We've sealed it for now," Fred said. "We have the girl's
appointment book. I'll give you a receipt for anything we
take."

Viola looked at him with hostile eyes. Apparently she
wasn't going to forgive or forget his slight faux pas about
the obvious difference between her and Mandi.

"No problem," she said coldly. "My life is an open book.
Take what you like."

Danny said, "We'll need to talk to you about Mandi."

"Not now, darling, please," Viola said. She contrived to
look helpless and distraught, but she was rather too imposing to pull it off. "I am too, *too* upset."

"We understand, ma'am. Actually . . ." the detective hesitated. "We'll need a positive identification."

Manicured hand to breast: "Me? I couldn't look at her.
She was a beautiful child. I want to remember her that way.
Such promise. She had ambition, beauty, sex appeal, wore
clothes very well indeed. She *loved* the money and she had
very little common sense, so she had all the qualifications
for going straight to the top. What a horrible thing I've
done to her."

The detectives leaned toward her, very interested now.

"I don't mean *I* killed her," Viola Roman said, and
frowned. "How silly of you to imagine that. I scarcely

knew the girl. But I put her in harm's way, since I more or less got her started in the business by introducing her to Rosellen Hamilton. She used to be a model, too, but now she has her own modeling agency with her husband." Viola sniffed. "Not as successful as they claim to be."

"They'd know about Mandi's private life though."

"I doubt it very much. They pay *no* attention to their girls. No, I wouldn't even bother with Rosellen. She'll tell you lies about how grand she was, how grand she is now."

They leaned back. Viola Roman leaned back as well and closed her eyes. She stroked the cat, which continued to glower at the two men.

"I was once a very famous woman," she said. "People remember me. I do hope the press doesn't get wind of this murder. The tabloids would certainly be after me. . . ."

"If you feel you'll be troubled, ma'am," Fred said innocently, "you should stay someplace secure. Do you have friends?"

"Certainly I have friends." Viola Roman opened her eyes and spoke haughtily. "But I'll stay at the Plaza. A fine hotel is so safe, don't you think? They have security men around." She smiled at the detectives. "Could you bring me the cat carrier? It's upstairs in the closet in the kitchen, on the floor. And bring my portfolio. It's a big black leather case beside the door."

She fluttered her thick, dark, and possibly false eyelashes. The cat in her lap tucked its feet under its plump body. "I won't leave poor little Tina behind, not ever again. And my precious will have bowls of shrimp to make it up to her."

"We'll drive you to the hotel," Danny said. The Plaza was only over on Fifth, a couple of dozen short blocks downtown.

Viola Roman said quickly, "Don't trouble. My car is double-parked right outside on the street." Suddenly she smiled, and Danny at least appreciated the glimpse of her former great beauty. "I hope you won't arrest me for that. I was planning to bring in my bag and then take the car around to the garage. Then I found out about this awful murder thing."

"You'll have to tell us where you were the last few days," Danny said offhandedly. "A formality."

Viola said, "I was staying with a darling old friend in New Jersey. A great fashion photographer until his eyesight went. I'll give you his number later. My address book is in the car. In the excitement over this murder, I left everything in the car."

The two detectives exchanged glances.

"We'll come around and pick you up after you have . . . settled yourself," Fred said. "How can we reach you?"

"The Plaza's in the phone book," Viola Roman said. "I don't carry the number around in my head." Then, to prove her point, she used the manager's phone to get the Plaza's number from information, and then called to book a room.

The cat carrier and portfolio were retrieved from the apartment, and the oversize Tina was deposited in the carrier. The detectives walked Viola to her car, which was indeed double-parked on the street but had as yet failed to attract a traffic agent with a ticket.

"Don't worry," Viola Roman said. "I'll keep to my room until I hear from you." She spoke directly to Danny. "I won't answer the door to anyone. . . ."

"I don't know that danger is that imminent," Danny said.

Viola opened her lovely eyes wide and put her hand to her brow in a graceful, dramatic gesture. "*Of course* it is! Until tomorrow."

Danny Nealon saw an almost sly smile as Viola drove away.

"You notice she didn't ask for any clothes from her apartment?" Fred said. "They usually want some of their things."

Danny said, "Maybe she has enough from her visit to New Jersey to carry her through a couple days at the Plaza. She's still something, isn't she?"

Fred shrugged. "She'll keep until morning, and so will this Rosellen. Roman doesn't want us to talk to her."

"But we will, and we'll start checking out the guys in Mandi's book and the names I found in the desk," Danny said.

"I want to go home," Fred said. "I got a feeling this will solve itself."

CHAPTER 5

PLAN AHEAD, that had always been Betty's motto. Leave little to chance. Expect delays. If experience had taught you that the copier invariably broke down the day after the maintenance contract expired, then you made certain that the maintenance contract was renewed well in advance. If you knew the fax machine always ran out of paper in the middle of the night when a long, important fax was coming through from the Edwards & Son distributor in Europe, you replaced the roll before you went home.

She'd set out earlier than necessary for the Winfield farm, to be sure she knew where she was supposed to be at seven. Once she'd found the place, she could retreat until the appointed hour.

It was nearly dark as Betty traveled along Timberhill Road. She'd driven in this direction only a few times, since the road meandered to nowhere she had ever needed to go. There were some newish ranch-style houses here and there, and once she had to stop for the flashing lights of a yellow school bus that was picking up a gaggle of children laden down with backpacks under the watchful eye of the day's designated mother-on-bus-stop-duty. Alida's big old house was set far back from the road and surrounded by stately trees, a sort of transplanted antebellum house that nobody except Alida would consider worth heating during a New England winter.

Betty was concentrating so much on the old days at Edwards & Son that she almost missed the turn to the Winfield farm. There was a big, bold number on the new mailbox on the corner, just as she'd been told, but no name. Mr. Crispin Abbott apparently didn't care to advertise his presence.

The old road was not inviting. It was ill paved with pot-holed tarmac. Not much renovation had been done here. In the deepening darkness she could make out low tumble-down fences made of loose gray rocks lining the road on either side. It seemed to her that there had once been well-tilled fields beyond the fences, but rampant grass and scrawny bushes had taken over.

A hundred yards down the road she glimpsed a small and very old cemetery on her left. A dozen mossy slabs of stone with eroded lettering were placed in rows. Some of the headstones were tilted. One had fallen over.

Betty had twenty minutes before she was due at the Winfield farm. She got out of her car and made her way to the stone barrier and peered into the cemetery. On the stone closest to her, the dates were the 1800s, the name was Winfield. The woman had died young.

The Cattonville of Betty's youth had had a similar cemetery, where the town founders, Yankees all, had been buried. Her own parents were buried in the Catholic cemetery in the next town.

Betty got back in her car and continued along the derelict road, which began to climb a slight hill. Around a bend she came upon a brand-new high and hostile chain-link fence with a wide double gate across the drive and some kind of electronic device locking it shut. There was a spotlight on the gate, and she could see lights up ahead, a glimpse of a roof, and part of the driveway in front of the house.

Betty got out of her car and examined the intercom box attached to the gate. It seemed simple enough, and she pressed the button she thought would sound in the house.

After a moment, a female voice said, "Who is it?"

"Elizabeth Trenka. I have an appointment with Mr. Abbott."

"Drive through when the gates open," the voice said. "They'll close after you."

The gates began to open slowly and silently. Betty drove through and on up the roadway which was now well paved. She came upon a splendid-looking stone and timber house, with a flagstone chimney and an expansion of modern additions and outbuildings. The old farmhouse per se had been swept away by a horde of latter-day architects. Muted spotlights hidden among the trees made the house appear to be in pale sunlight. The house was cozily landscaped, and Betty imagined that the old farmland stretched on beyond it to the low hills that bounded the far side of East Moulton township. No lights of other houses could be seen from where she stood in the driveway, at exactly two minutes to seven.

A rather large canine creature approached diffidently.

Ah, she thought, the dog that I should not be frightened by. It was not the Doberman or Alsatian watchdog of her experience but of a similar configuration. It had a raised line of fur along its back. She groped for a name. Rhodesian ridgeback. An expensive dog. Another one appeared.

They seemed friendly enough, if aloof. They came closer and circled her, eyeing her curiously.

"Go away," Betty said kindly but firmly. She saw them as rather like persistent yet amiable office-supply salesmen from whom one had no intention of purchasing even a single number two pencil.

The dogs went away.

Betty examined the huge door knocker in the shape of a lion with a ring in its jaws. Then she prepared to meet Crispin Abbott, whoever he might be. Somehow she was sure he would make it clear to her exactly who he thought he was.

Betty grasped the ring in the lion's mouth and let it fall with a thump.

The door opened almost immediately.

The tall young woman who stood before her was somewhat at odds with Betty's mental picture of a country estate. She had very long, straight blond hair and a tiny turquoise bikini better suited to the beaches of the Côte d'Azur at midday than an autumn evening in East Moulton.

"Elizabeth Trenka," Betty said, looking surreptitiously at the looped gold ring piercing the young woman's navel. Then she looked at the girl's face. It was vaguely familiar.

"He's expecting you," the young woman said. "Come in. It's freezing out. I'm Sonia. We kind of ran into each other today at the supermarket."

"Of course," Betty said. It was the person Betty had believed was a glamorous East Moulton housewife. She followed Sonia into an aggressively colonial-style room with a plethora of wooden rockers and braided rugs topped off by a fireplace with all manner of brass bowls and iron pots, fire dogs, and pokers. Only a spinning wheel and butter churn were lacking.

"You may have to wait," Sonia said dreamily. "He's going over some business with our so-called housekeeper. I'm sure she drinks. Crispin claims he's a genius, so people have to make allowances." She giggled. "Don't let him bully you. He's bullied me to the end of my rope. If you want to escape fast, a release button is on the right-hand gate near the ground."

Betty took one of the uncomfortable-looking rockers. "Your father?" she asked hesitantly.

Sonia's laugh was hollow. "Thank goodness, no. He is my patron. I am his muse. Sometimes I pose for him, and sometimes I just keep him company while he talks and talks. He likes to think we're all one big cozy family, but we're just an entourage." She giggled again, and Betty wondered if she'd been enjoying the cocktail hour in her tiny bathing costume. "And entourages don't have much loyalty, do they? I'm really an actress, and I can't wait to get back to good old Manhattan. Or maybe I'll head for Hollywood. This place is creepy ... that cemetery down the drive and these black nights, with no lights from any houses except way off through the trees. No people, nothing to do. The town is pretty awful—oops, sorry!" She swayed slightly. "You live here."

"I'm new in town," Betty said. "No offense taken."

"I don't like the company Crispin keeps. That thug, and I don't care how gorgeous he thinks he is. And his mother! I'm the only one who sees what's going on. Crispin doesn't, or he doesn't care. It's like living in a Tennessee Williams play without the southern accent." Sonia seemed bent on voicing her complaints to a stranger. She looked Betty over, seeming slightly unfocused. Several cocktails perhaps. "Crispin will find himself a muse to replace me easily enough, but . . ."

"Not me, surely," Betty said.

"He doesn't know that yet, does he?" Sonia was amused. "He's already seen another applicant. You've got to know her, the girl who works in the supermarket. She was here only a few minutes, and tore off like the devil was after her. I think the thug scared her off." Sonia shrugged. "He can always get someone from New York. This place sounds good on paper. Go through that door when he yells for you. It's more comfortable in his studio than this awful room. I'm going to take a swim."

"It seems the wrong season for swimming," Betty said.

"Crispin had a fabulous indoor pool put in. He's totally extravagant. It's part of his charm." She tiptoed away across the broad-planked wood floor, opened a door, and disappeared.

"Patron" and "muse," Betty thought, were imaginative names for whatever role Crispin Abbott saw himself in relation to his young women like the fairly sophisticated Sonia.

But Carole? For all her brave makeup, she was really a small-town girl. No wonder she'd fled.

The room was rather warm, but Betty decided against removing her trench coat. Crispin Abbott's genius might prove too much for her. She wanted to be prepared for a rapid departure.

A snuffling sound heralded the reappearance of the ridgebacks, or possibly two more. They came from a darkened hallway through an arched entrance and stopped at the sight of her in the rocker. One of them raised its muzzle and sniffed. Then the two dogs flopped on the largest oval braided rug and closed their eyes. Apparently Betty was acceptable to them.

She heard the front door opening, but the person who appeared was not anyone's patron, rather, a muscular young man with a leather jacket slung over his shoulder. His T-shirt showed well-developed biceps and chest as though he frequently worked out to improve his physique. His long, dark hair was tied back in a ponytail, and there was a tiny diamond stud in his left ear. He had startlingly blue eyes.

Earrings, navel rings, colonial fire dogs, and leather jackets. Winfield Farm was nothing if not trendy. Could the designer spring water be far behind?

Betty thought the young man remarkably good-looking, but his expression was surly. The two dogs raised their heads, a tail thumped on the floor, and they returned to their nap. The man was obviously a familiar sight. He stared at Betty for a moment, and then went to the door Sonia had indicated led to Crispin Abbott's inner sanctum and entered without knocking. It closed behind him with a solid thunk.

Betty tried to ignore the rather loud voices that now came from Abbott's room. Masculine rumblings and a woman's voice, high-pitched and complaining. Then there was silence. The door was flung open suddenly, and the young man emerged, followed by a plumpish, dowdy woman carrying a coat. Both were scowling. The woman looked familiar, someone she had seen in town or at the library perhaps. The woman stamped through the door Sonia had taken while the young man stayed behind, eyeing Betty suspiciously. Then he hurled himself into the rocker opposite hers.

"Where is she?" a voice boomed out. "Where's my new girl?"

Feeling not at all girlish, Betty stood up and looked at the person who had opened the door of the studio. The extremely ugly man before her was fairly short and squat with white hair cut to barely a half inch and noticeably large ears. If there was any doubt that he was the master there, the dogs erased it as both leapt to their feet and bounded toward him, tongues lolling.

Betty thought he resembled Erich von Stroheim, only not quite so appealing. His nose seemed to have been broken more than once, and there was a scar on one cheek, although it did not seem to be the traditional dueling scar beloved of the Prussian military caste. The paint-spattered sweatshirt and baggy dark-blue drawstring pants over very high-tech athletic shoes completed the startling picture of the resident genius.

He seemed somewhat taken aback at the sight of his "girl," but recovered gracefully.

"You are exactly as I imagined," Crispin Abbott said without truth. He patted the slavering dogs' heads absentmindedly. "A strong, competent woman who will not bend to my will at the first gruff word. Someone who sees the depths behind the façade and will type my words without making judgments . . ."

Oh, really! Betty thought. Shall I manage to keep a straight face?

"I am not here to judge," Betty said, and thought she sounded quite as nonsensical as he.

"Come away from this terrible room," Abbott said. "I succumbed to my interior designer's vision. She was extraordinarily attractive and she loved the colonial style, so I indulged her." He sighed. "She was not as talented as she was good-looking, alas. It's much more pleasant in my studio." He opened the door and turned back to the young man who still glowered beside the fireplace. "Take the dogs out for a run," Abbott commanded. "And quit looking so aggrieved. You have to pay back something for a safe haven and good meals."

Crispin Abbott ushered Betty into his studio.

"Let me take your coat," Abbott said as he closed the door behind them. "Sonia is in many ways an angel, but she has minimal manners. I sometimes wonder if superior mammary development saps common sense."

Betty opened her mouth to argue Abbott's crude sexism, then decided it was not her business to argue with someone who might be a genius, although no sign of it had yet made itself obvious.

"Sonia's had her problems," he said. "I thought this place would be good for her."

He helped her out of her coat. Betty was many inches taller than he. Short men usually disliked being looked down on by their typists, but he apparently was at ease.

The studio was a huge room that appeared to have been added on to the original farmhouse. One wall was entirely windows. Now it faced the night, but Betty was confident that Crispin Abbott had arranged to have a splendid daytime view of colorful hills and sloping lawns. Scattered about the room were easels with half-finished paintings, including a number of nude women, globs of shapeless clay on stands, a potter's wheel, worktables covered with big sheets of paper with bold abstract charcoal scrawls. On one side of the room was a grouping of big, puffy red-and-black leather chairs and couches. On the walls were hung displays of ethnic art: African masks, a feather cape, a clutter of machetes, spears, and arrows. A wall of open shelves held piles of brilliantly colored fabrics, a medley of antique toys, an array of wineglasses and vases in deep primary colors.

"How interesting," Betty said.

"Merely amusing," Crispin Abbott said. "I have much better things elsewhere. Take a seat. Ah, not that chair. This one is much more comfortable. Coffee? Tea? I keep champagne chilled. Nothing?"

He appeared to be close to Betty's age. He might be a true eccentric, or . . .

"I am, Miss Trenka, a Renaissance man," he said almost humbly, as though he bore the burden bravely.

"That answers my question," Betty said. She had a sudden recollection of his name in connection with a nasty lawsuit. Or it might have been a divorce involving a lot of money. Whatever, she seemed to recall that Crispin Abbott had come out ahead of the game. A man not to be trifled with.

"I am writing my autobiography," Crispin Abbott said. "In longhand, on yellow lined legal pads. I intend to have it privately and expensively published, rather the way T. E. Lawrence published *The Seven Pillars of Wisdom*. No talk shows, no newspaper interviews, no movie of the week. Only a select few will read it now. I owe my life to posterity, not to the immediate present."

How clever, Betty thought. By making his autobiography highly inaccessible, everyone will want to read it. "And you would like to hire me to type your words for the printer?" she asked.

"Exactly! You understand that it is highly confidential. Naturally, I have enemies who would like to get a look at it, so I need an ally I can trust absolutely. You, my dear lady, are a person sent by the gods. I knew instinctively that you were a rare creature indeed.

Good grief, Betty thought. If the typist is showered with flattery, what must the muse have to endure?

"Would you want me to work here?" she asked cautiously.

"Heavens no. Can you do the work at your home?"

"Yes," Betty said with perhaps too obvious relief.

"I require no editing," he said airily, "although I would be grateful if you would consult with me on possible misspellings. Historical dates? I can never keep the sequence of presidents in mind, although I've met them all. My schooling was erratic. I will pay you a hundred dollars a day for every day that I engage you, whether or not there is anything to type."

"Two hundred," Betty said promptly. "I couldn't do it for less."

"Aha! A hundred and fifty, then. When I hand you material, you will work a seven-hour day. And I don't care which seven hours you choose to work. If there are days when you have nothing to type, you will still be paid. It may take some time. The manuscript is not completed." He grinned engagingly, which made him look almost attractive. "And I am making revisions. I want my life to sound exactly right."

"I see," Betty said. The job sounded too good to be true, and she had always warned the girls at the office that if something sounded too good to be true, it usually was, but she hadn't figured out the catch yet. "I will accept your offer on a limited basis. The fee is ample, but I will undertake the job for two weeks, at which time we both have the option of canceling or continuing our association."

"Hah! I knew my instincts were right. The minute I saw you, I knew you had brains. Tall women have to in order to survive, especially those beyond the blush of youth."

Betty said amiably, "I have found that short men think they gain stature by being insulting."

Crispin Abbott stared at her, and then roared with laughter. "Good work," he said. "Let me write you a check for our first two weeks of blissful togetherness."

He went to his worktable and rummaged through papers until he found a checkbook.

"I'll start tomorrow," Betty said.

"Excellent." He paused in writing out the check and gazed at her. "You're wondering about my household."

"Not at all," Betty said quickly, but in truth she was. A muse, a youth, a dowdy woman, and the genius.

"Dear Sonia has been my model," he said, "but she persists in saying she's an actress. She'd like to marry a large pile of money. She'll be disappointed, I fear. She's not happy here, so she's leaving in a week or so." He shook his head and returned to the check.

"That young man . . ." Betty began.

"He comes across as an attractive thug, doesn't he? I suppose he is. I met him in New York when he was on the brink of some awful trouble. . . . It's a long story, but he just recently turned up here. He's good with the dogs, being a country boy." Abbott handed her the check.

"Doesn't he worry you?"

Abbott laughed. "Harmless. All surly silences and dark looks. His mother's looking after the house for the moment, but she's not adequate. I can't fire her yet, until I replace Sonia." He gazed at Betty.

"And you were hoping that I . . . ?" Betty laughed in spite of herself and in spite of what Sonia had already hinted.

Abbott looked at her, then chuckled. "You're on to me."

"I understand you interviewed an acquaintance of mine," Betty said boldly. "Carole."

"Yes. Not suitable at all," he said shortly, then added, "I guarantee you'll find the story of my life absolutely engrossing."

"And absolutely true, I'm certain," Betty said. She knew she was being half seduced by his peculiar charm.

"Only I know that, dear lady. What should I call you? Miss Trenka sounds so . . . so . . ."

"Elizabeth?"

Abbott shook his head. "I had a wife named Elizabeth once. Betty will do, what do you say?" There was nothing Betty could say. He opened the door to the colonial room. The dogs leapt to their feet, eager for attention from the master. Betty saw the young man still rocking slowly back and forth in the chair before the fireplace.

Crispin said, "Miss Trenka is going to be working for me. See that you treat her well. Betty, this is Johnny Fender."

Somehow, Betty was not terribly surprised. Johnny said nothing as Crispin said to Betty, "Let me show you a bit of my house, if you have the time. I did a superb job. It was a terrible old ruin when I was put on to it." He turned to the young man. "Isn't that right?"

The young man stood up. "I'm taking the pickup to town to see somebody," he said.

"Is that wise?" Abbott said.

"It doesn't matter." Johnny stalked out. Betty had the feeling that he'd been waiting for her to reappear and leave.

She didn't like him one bit. He was trouble. She knew things as instinctively as Crispin Abbott claimed to.

Abbott guided her to the door Sonia had taken and said in a low voice, "Difficult, that one. He reminds me of me when I was that age. Rebellious, troubled, and living on the brink of disaster."

"Then perhaps you'd do well to reconsider having him here," Betty said.

"He's been useful," Crispin Abbott said. "I'll get rid of him when it's more convenient."

The rapid tour of Abbott's house took them down long hallways with glimpses of huge bedrooms; it brought them downstairs to an idyllic pool room tucked away in the basement, paneled in dark wood with couches, potted palms, a bar, and Oriental rugs around the perimeter of the pool. Sonia was floating lazily in the center of the green water. She ignored them.

They looked in on a well-equipped gym, admired paintings and sculptures, not all of them from the hand of Crispin Abbott, he assured her. He pointed out cases of exquisite pre-Columbian artworks, certainly made of gold, but apparently unprotected. She viewed a vast, shining kitchen, with professional-looking ranges and ovens, a colossal dining room fitted out with a long refectory table, and several sitting rooms in different styles.

"Not much of the old house remains," Abbott said as they again reached the front door. "Indeed, except for the outlines and some of the old wooden floors and that cemetery down the hill, the crew I brought in pretty much redid the whole place. Give me a call in a day or two, tell me how it's going. Confidential, remember. But you're new to the town, so you won't have that many people to gossip with. I'll see that the gates open when you reach them."

"Good evening, Mr. Abbott," Betty said. "I'll keep everything quiet." Then she added, "And I certainly won't tell my neighbors what you've created out of the old house. They'd be lining up for tours."

Abbott looked thoughtful. "For a modest entrance

fee . . ." Then he grinned and actually looked quite appealing. "At a later time, perhaps."

He stood at the front door and watched her get into her car.

Betty drove away slowly. The sturdy gates swung open as she approached, and she saw them close behind her in the rearview mirror.

How did Crispin Abbott know that she was new in town? How did his notice get posted at the top of the bulletin board? Sonia or someone else must have pinned it up; Crispin Abbott could not have reached that high. He hadn't asked a thing about her qualifications. How did he know she could do what she promised for a rather large amount of money? Why were Johnny Fender and his mother there? She shook her head. Poor Carole.

The questions troubled her a little, as did the atmosphere at the Winfield farm. She could sense the tensions.

The fat envelope with the beginning of Crispin Abbott's autobiography rested on the seat beside her. She might not have been what he had hoped for, but he perhaps had decided on the spot that a typist in hand was preferable to no typist at all. The book could be more interesting fiction than many television programs she'd seen lately.

As she passed the old cemetery, she slowed and peered out the side window. If she was not mistaken, a pickup truck was parked in a dark lane, lights off and no one visible. She speeded up in spite of the rutted surface of the road, and turned onto Timberhill Road. The truck with Johnny in it, if that's what it was, didn't follow her, since she saw no headlights in the rearview mirror as she headed homeward.

Then she mentally kicked herself for becoming melodramatic. She should rather be thinking about a quiet supper, a good night's sleep, and getting to work the next day in her peaceful house on Timberhill Road.

Betty ate her dinner with Crispin Abbott's manuscript on the table beside her. He had truly written out his autobiography in longhand on yellow lined legal pads. Happily, his handwriting was the same precise italic that had been used for his notice in the supermarket. She scanned through the manuscript to get an idea of his quirks and style. It was unlikely that one comparatively unattractive man could have achieved so many romantic conquests, reached such heights of artistic acclaim, and known so many persons of world-class significance (and intimately, too) in one lifetime. She wondered approximately what percentage of all this was true. Her guess was on the low side. On the other hand, at her meeting she'd ended up being mildly charmed by him, so perhaps others were also drawn to him.

"I was born and raised in a small town eight miles from the top of the Alleghenies," Crispin Abbott's manuscript began. "At least that is what I tell people who ask. The truth is somewhat different. Think Palm Beach, think Versailles. Think Buckingham Palace. Think anything you choose, because the story of my life begins not with my sad and lonely infancy and boyhood, but with my sudden dazzling appearance on the New York artistic and literary scene in the 1950s."

Betty was going to be thoroughly entertained by Crispin Abbott's memories.

She put down chapter one, page one, to answer the ringing phone.

"Have you read any of it? What do you think?"

"Mr. Abbott? Really, I've had it for only an hour or so. I glanced at it to be sure I could read your handwriting."

"That's no problem. I pride myself— But what did you think?"

"I'm certain I will find it engrossing," Betty said cautiously. She wasn't sure how opinionated the typist should be about the content of a manuscript.

"There aren't many I can discuss it with," Crispin Abbott said, "since almost everyone I know is in it. Go on . . ."

"Mr. Abbott, I don't quite know what to say at this early stage."

"To start, Betty, you should call me Crispin. I do trust your judgment."

Betty thought he had little basis for trusting her in any matter, except perhaps to show up for an appointment on time. She said, "My judgment is that it's too soon to offer an opinion. It . . . it wouldn't be fair to your work."

"Very astute," Crispin Abbott said. "I knew at once you were a woman of remarkable character. Most people would have fawned. Sonia fawned over the first chapter, in the days when she was eager to please me. Now she sulks. Off in her room sulking right now, I don't doubt, when I need company, conversation . . ."

Aha, Betty thought, the man is lonely and thinks he's discovered a new source of entertainment in his typist. She could manage to be kind, since she knew what it meant to be alone, although until her retirement she'd never felt really lonely.

"You must be accustomed to a more lively life than what East Moulton and the farm offer," she said. "Perhaps you should be inviting your friends from New York to visit."

"I plan to, definitely," he said. "I've only just got the house fixed to my satisfaction, and I need better help. Maybe you know a nice, agreeable local woman . . . and a man to handle the grounds and buildings. I have to concentrate on my work. The Fenders seem to think they own the place."

So Crispin Abbott was not happy with his housekeeper, who drank, according to Sonia, and her surly son, who was not welcome in East Moulton. Betty said, "I'll ask around."

"I should mix more with my new neighbors," he said, "but I don't like leaving the house until I have reliable people. I have some valuable art here. Now, as soon as you've had a chance to read the manuscript more carefully . . . My whole life is there."

"This is what I will do," Betty said firmly. She did not wish to become Crispin Abbott's Best Friend. "I'll call you tomorrow after I've read a bit more. We'll discuss it then."

"That's my girl."

Oh, please, Betty thought. My girlhood is long gone. "Until tomorrow, Mr. Abbott . . . Crispin."

She'd become a Reader/Adviser. Perhaps she should have one of those neon signs in her window the way palm readers and fortune-tellers do.

CHAPTER 6

"ELIZABETH ANNE Trenka, this is your life!"

Betty said, "Mmmm," but it seemed a terrible effort to open her eyes. And why was that ancient TV show haunting her awake and sleeping? Her left arm prickled when she moved it. She'd fallen asleep on the couch once again with her arm half under her body.

"Your life. Your life."

Now she did open one eye. The large television set across from the sofa flickered bright colors in the darkened room. A blond woman in a clinging red gown extolled the virtues of . . . something.

"*Your* life *your* life . . ."

It wasn't the woman on the TV talking. Betty's phone was ringing. She sat up abruptly and felt a little dizzy. The prickles in her arm surged, then subsided.

She reached out and grabbed the receiver.

Whatever could I have been dreaming about? she wondered. Surely mature women do not dream about having their lives exposed on a long-departed TV show.

"Hello?" It was a croak rather than her normal voice. "Hello?" she said again, and this time sounded more like a professional office manager, even if she no longer had an office to manage.

"Is this Betty Trenka from Cattonville?" It was a woman's voice, breathless and faint.

Cattonville? Betty had moved from the town of her birth in northwestern Connecticut forty-two years ago, at the age of twenty-one. After she had buried her mother two decades ago, she had never returned.

"Yes," Betty said warily. "Who is this?"

"You live in East Moulton now." It was a statement.

"Who is speaking?" Betty was not easily unsettled, but she didn't care for this, especially in view of that strange earlier call. Her house on Timberhill Road was not all that well protected by neighbors.

"It's Viola," the woman said. There was a nervous edge to her voice. "Viola Romanowski. You remember. The brown house on Maple Street."

"Viola!" Betty was flabbergasted. "I thought of you only today. How did you find me?"

Viola didn't respond to that. Instead, she said, "I'm on the Connecticut Turnpike past New Haven. I can be at your place in an hour."

"It's rather late," Betty said. The mantelpiece clock she'd received on her reluctant retirement said nine-thirty. She'd wanted to get to bed early to be up with the dawn to start on Crispin Abbott's manuscript.

"Betty, I need help. For old time's sake. I don't have anyone else to turn to. I'll stay only the night."

"Well ..." Betty wasn't sure she had time for this, and then she shrugged. She did. "What's the problem, Viola?"

"I had to get out of New York in a hurry. I need a place where nobody will find me for a day or so." Viola sounded close to the edge of hysteria. "They got Mandi, and now they're after me."

"Who are they? Who is Mandi?"

"I'll explain when I get there. I don't want to be murdered in my sleep."

Mandi? Murder? They? Betty might have the time, but she did not really have the inclination to entertain an apparently deranged person from her distant past.

Viola half sobbed. "Please ..."

"All right," Betty said reluctantly. Viola seemed to be losing her grip. "I live on Timberhill Road. It's about a mile west of the town center. On the left, three blue spruces in front. I'll leave the front light on."

"An hour," Viola said. "I can find you. Don't say a word about me to anyone. I don't want to spoil the story." The phone went dead.

Betty replaced the receiver slowly in its cradle. Another person who demanded confidentiality.

Of course she remembered Viola Romanowski from Cattonville, the small upstate Connecticut factory town where she'd been born and raised. Of course she remembered the brown house on Maple Street, full of Romanowski children, from lanky, blond Viola, three or four years younger than herself, down in regular steps to little Joey the baby.

She remembered that as a teenager Viola couldn't seem to keep out of the scrapes that the whole town talked about—the boyfriends nobody approved of, trouble with teachers, the times she ran away and returned with tales of marvelous adventures and great excuses that sometimes bordered on fantasy.

"That girl will come to no good end" was a fairly constant comment from Betty's mother. "She's too cute for her own good. And wild. You should have heard the whopper she told her ma about how she managed to get all the way to Hartford without a dime in her pocket to meet some GI back from overseas."

World War II and its aftermath had provided considerable opportunities for socializing for girls like Viola. Not so much for girls like Betty, the ones who were tall and awkward, serious and not "cute."

I really envied Viola back then, she thought wryly. That carefree approach to life was not something Pop allowed.

How had Viola found her after all these years? Why? And exactly who should Betty not say "a word" to? What story?

The tale of pursuit by killers was simply too preposterous. Betty sighed. Perhaps Viola's habit of getting into scrapes and telling wonderful tales had never been conquered.

If Viola were staying the night, Betty would have to put clean sheets on the bed in the upstairs guest room.

The program on Betty's big-screen TV babbled on, punctuated by hearty artificial laughter, but Betty's mind was still back in the old hometown.

Viola had left Cattonville for good at seventeen or eighteen, about the same time Betty had. Betty finished secretarial school and was glad to find a job at a small manufacturing company near Bristol. The high-paying wartime factory jobs for women had already vanished. She was happy to have a job at all. Her father thought a girl should get married to a nice local boy and keep a nice house like her mother. Betty never had the courage to tell Pop that since no nice boy from town ever asked, she wasn't about to live out her life as Cattonville's spinster. Later, she found her permanent niche at Edwards & Son, and remained there for thirty-seven years.

Betty paused in tucking in the top sheet. There had been some temporary and difficult niches along the way. She shook her head to drive away those memories.

Viola was a different story. Her eyes had been on the glamour of distant places and their beautiful people. Sure enough, by the 1950s, Viola Romanowski had reached New York a memorable woman with a single name: Violetta. Almost the face of the decade, but not quite, since she was competing with the likes of Dovima, Dorian Leigh, Suzy Parker, and Wilhelmina. All the same, Violetta had stared out haughtily at Betty for years from the covers of *Vogue* and *Harper's Bazaar*. The lanky body had been turned into the perfect framework for the slim Dior New Look fashions: tiny waist, narrow jutting hips, haughtily elegant from her swanlike neck to her carefully placed feet. Perfect hair that never moved in the wind; perfect makeup that never smeared; perfectly unreal. Lesser women emulated her, thanks to those horrendous foundation garments that produced a smooth, long line on the outside but considerable physical anguish for those incorrectly shaped by nature for the fashions of the time.

More than once through the years Betty had lingered at magazine stands, and surreptitiously leafed through the pages of fashion magazines she couldn't afford for a glimpse of Viola. Betty was tall herself, but no one ever suggested that she try to be a model. No one ever suggested that Betty Trenka could wear the high-fashion clothes that looked so exquisite on Violetta. Betty had often envied the life she imagined Violetta led, in contrast to the sordid intrigues of the steno pool, the tyranny of carbon paper, and the domineering bluster of the men she served loyally.

Betty hoped Viola wouldn't mind the pile of unpacked cartons in the corner of the guest room. She had plenty of clean towels, but would a formerly famous fashion model have a problem with sharing the bathroom with a never-famous childhood friend?

She got out an extra blanket against the autumn chill.

Betty's father died in a factory accident and soon her mother was gone as well. Viola/Violetta, too, disappeared from the covers of *Vogue*, the success that had burned so brightly for a decade snuffed out by age. She was forgotten at thirty, although Betty remembered her from time to time, as she had today looking at Carole at her cash register, so eager for a better, more glamorous life than a small town could offer.

Betty frowned. Viola's situation today wasn't much different from Betty's—only Viola's "retirement" had happened a long time before. Viola would be nearing sixty, her career over half her lifetime ago. What had she been up to since then?

It was nearly eleven. Viola believed she'd be in quiet East Moulton in an hour, but she couldn't know exactly where Timberhill Road was, so she'd be much longer. Few people were abroad at night in the town to give directions. Indeed, only the bar and grill on Main Street stayed open beyond eleven o'clock, and then, people joked, only if the four or five regulars decided to pay the bartender extra to stick around for one more beer and the end of a sports event on television.

Upstairs in her own room at the front of the house, Betty saw that there were no lights at the Saks house across the field. With those three boys, Penny and Greg tended to retire early. The light was on over the front door of Ted Kelso's low stone house across Timberhill Road, now that he was safely back from Boston.

Boston.

Betty's cousin Rita lived in Boston. She had been closer to Viola in age than Betty. Indeed, Betty seemed to recall that Rita had made a passing reference to Viola half a dozen years or more ago, when they'd been reminiscing about Cattonville days on one of their rare get-togethers. Rita had run into her or gotten a letter or something. She could well have stayed in touch with Viola, and of course Rita had Betty's new address. Therefore, Betty concluded, Rita could have told Viola where she was now living.

It could be a totally false conclusion, but Betty could now put aside the puzzle of how and consider the reason why.

The why of Viola Romanowski, the once-glamorous— and now possibly mad—Violetta, was mildly intriguing. Having her overnight probably wouldn't be all that terrible. Her work for Crispin Abbott might be delayed a bit, but she could make it up after Viola was gone.

The dormer window in the guest room looked out on the backyard and the old garage. As she slid the pillows into cases, a flash, a car's high beams perhaps, made it appear that a light had been turned on and off quickly inside the garage, below the dusty panes along the top of the double doors. It happened so quickly that she might have imagined it.

She watched for a moment, but the light did not return.

Betty went back downstairs to her television set to watch the eleven o'clock news and hope that she wouldn't doze off again. Years of regular habits, up at dawn, in bed by ten-thirty at the latest, with the next day's clothes for the office laid out hadn't prepared her for late-night vigils for someone who needed her help, in fact or in fantasy.

As she settled down on the sofa, she had to admit rue-fully that she liked being needed, even by the likes of Viola, and especially now, when no one appeared to need her at all anymore, not even Carole. Well, Crispin Abbott needed her, but he was paying well for the privilege.

"You need to feel indispensable," Sid Edwards Senior had told her some twenty years before. "You like it. It's going to get you in trouble someday."

Betty remembered that she'd looked at Sid, he in his mid-fifties and as handsome and distinguished as the day she'd come to work for him, and she already into her forties.

She'd wanted to say to him: "It already has," but she said instead, "I've never regretted one thing, Sid," and left it at that.

Sid Senior had said, almost too softly to be heard clearly, "Neither have I."

Betty tried never to think of her old personal attachments, only the professional ones. She had made choices that weren't always good ones, and she'd lived with them, but she didn't dwell on them.

The hands on her retirement clock continued to mark off the closing minutes of what had started out to be another quiet day of retirement—until Crispin Abbott had appeared in her life and Viola had phoned.

She felt a bit resentful. Her first tentative steps into her uncertain future were being disrupted. That had never happened in the old days, where everything ran like clockwork if she had anything to say about it. People seldom intruded unexpectedly on her life outside of Edwards & Son.

It was too late to call Rita in Boston about Viola. The convent, such as it was, unplugged its phone early, and in any case, Sister Rita might be on duty at the homeless women's shelter the nuns ran.

She settled back to wait, still fitfully irritated, and then the damned phone rang again.

"Did I wake you?" It was Crispin Abbott, one more time.

"No, no, not at all." She waited to hear what now.

"I've been thinking, Betty. Could I have made a mistake in moving here? I thought I needed peace, a place for all my beautiful treasures. A place where I could work." He sounded quite uneasy. "Some nights I feel I'm past my prime."

"Nonsense," Betty said more sharply than she intended. "I'm retired, but I don't feel that way. Anyhow, artists don't retire." She couldn't bring herself to say that geniuses worked till their last breath. "Human beings don't retire, for heaven's sake. They just find new patterns for their lives." She had a mental picture of her imagined "Reader/Adviser" sign blinking on and off in the night.

"I'll let you go," Abbott said. "Sonia usually stays up late talking. I can't imagine what's made her so cross. Don't forget to call tomorrow about the manuscript."

"I promise," Betty said. "An unexpected houseguest is arriving any minute, so I may be a bit delayed in getting to work, but I'll make it up quickly. And yes, I will call."

If Viola could be headed off to bed at once without telling her tale in full and riotous detail until morning, Betty could get her sleep. She might still get some work in early on Crispin Abbott's manuscript. She imagined that Viola was the kind to sleep in.

"That's it, then," Crispin Abbott said.

"Yes," Betty said. "Good night."

CHAPTER 7

THE KNOCK on the door came after midnight.

Betty had fallen asleep again, this time sitting up, but she was immediately awake, and puzzled. She had a perfectly good doorbell at her front door, with the porch light to guide Viola, but the knocking—loud and urgent—was coming from the back door to the kitchen.

Betty approached the door cautiously in the dark, and peered out through its small square pane of glass. The person outside couldn't be anyone but Viola Romanowski.

Betty opened the door and Viola, forty years older than in Cattonville days, surged into the kitchen and dropped a handbag, a large black leather portfolio, and a old-fashioned square makeup case that popped open to scatter vials and tubes and jars across the blue-and-white tile floor.

"Viola, how nice to see . . ."

"Don't turn on a light," Viola gasped. "I don't want them to see me." She peered around the darkened kitchen. "Is anyone here?" She stooped to gather up her scattered possessions.

"Certainly not," Betty said. "Look, there's a lipstick or something there by the sink. Come along to the living room."

Viola hesitated in the act of dropping a handful of tiny brushes into the case. In the half light of the kitchen, she looked as elegant as in those long-ago haute couture layouts. A long, flared coat in electric blue concealed any alteration of her remembered willowy shape, but surely even the legendary Violetta couldn't escape the inroads of cruel gravity and weary skin. As far as Betty could tell, she was still blond, although her head was swathed in a copious dark blue chiffon scarf that trailed off behind her.

"Are the curtains drawn?" Viola breathed.

"Yes," Betty said, slightly alarmed by Viola's nervousness. "In a manner of speaking. The venetian blinds are down. I've only just moved here. I'm still planning my . . . my window treatment." Betty had learned the term from Penny Saks, who devoted a lot of time to reading interior decorating magazines. "Why on earth did you come to the back door? Didn't you park out front?"

"I didn't want them to see me arriving," Viola said. "I parked down the road and came across the field. We'll see about fetching my things later."

Oh, really, Betty thought. This is too much.

"Do you mean to say that someone is following you?" Betty didn't like the sound of that.

"One can't be too careful," Viola said evasively as she followed Betty to the living room. "I am still a story in my way."

The story again. Why did everyone have a story that couldn't be told quite yet? Betty turned on a second lamp. "Did you have trouble finding my place?"

"These little towns are no problem," Viola said.

"My friend Eugene Salzman had trouble even in broad daylight," Betty said.

"Actually, I stopped at a place when I came off the turnpike. A sort of roadhouse. Very lively. I spoke with some helpful young people about directions, and then it seemed"—she smiled brightly—"as though I'd been here before. Isn't it amazing?"

"Amazing," Betty said, "although Al's Good Times is not the most desirable spot for asking directions." What the proper town matrons said was that it was a sleazy dump and a danger to the morals of the community. She couldn't imagine the impact of an appearance by Violetta on Al's patrons.

"Utterly harmless, dear. New York has places much,

much worse that simply everyone adores." Viola looked around. "It's a rather small place you have." The voice of Viola suddenly became the voice of glamorous Violetta herself, accustomed to the luxury of spacious rooms and sweeping staircases.

"I hadn't thought that," Betty said.

"I'm sure it's just right for someone like you."

Betty briefly considered taking offense at this minor rudeness, but decided it was pointless. Viola had apparently donned her famous model persona, and there would doubtless be more significant rudeness to come, where taking offense would be more gratifying.

"Perhaps it will strike me as small after I've been here a while," Betty said.

"It's . . . cozy certainly. Now, let me look at you, darling!" Violetta had decided to play gracious lady, and put her hands on Betty's shoulders, and—as few others were able to do—looked Betty in the eye. "How well you look! After all these years!"

Betty looked back. She couldn't imagine what Viola saw when she looked at Betty, but to Betty the years had made definite, inevitable inroads on Viola's beauty. Even so, Viola was wearing lush, dark false eyelashes, and her makeup was flawless. Apparently her need to hide out from "them" had not prevented her from trying to look her best, even under trying circumstances.

Betty said, "You said something about a 'story' on the phone. You can't mean that the *press* is after you?" She was afraid that was exactly what Viola meant.

Viola dropped her coat on a chair and unwound the chiffon scarf. White blond hair in a stiff pageboy style. A sedate but chic black dress with pearls—too large surely to be real. Her waist was still narrow, but Betty could see the fine lines around her eyes. She wore astonishingly high heels—how had she managed to cross the field in the dark?

"Don't worry, darling. They can't have found me yet. We have time to prepare. Some of them pay quite well for an exclusive. Especially the tabloid television people. I brought my portfolio, just in case." She tapped the black leather case with her toe. "My old pictures are simply marvelous!"

"Viola, I don't really think I want to be involved . . ."

"It's *no* problem," Viola said. "Ah! My suitcase. I don't have much. I suppose the police thought the Plaza would send out for anything else I might need."

"The police! Viola, what *is* going on?" Betty had always thought of herself as eminently patient, but Viola was testing her greatly.

"I'm so sorry. I do owe you an explanation. While I was away from New York visiting a friend, a lovely young girl was murdered in my apartment. A really beautiful model from out of town who was staying with me. Paying me a bit for the space and my help. Even with rent control, everything helps. Although personally unpleasant as only young women can be, she was going to be a tremendous success. I found her. The sight of her body, horribly strangled, lying on the bedroom floor was . . . was *awful*." Viola shuddered, and collapsed on the sofa, overcome by the memory. "She was very careless about the friends she chose."

"I don't remember reading about it in the papers," Betty said, "or seeing it on television."

"They *just* found her today," Viola said.

Betty said sternly, "You just said that you found her."

"I *discovered* her," Viola said grandly, "for the business. They *found* her."

"And who did it?"

Viola hesitated. "I couldn't say."

"Couldn't or won't."

"Betty darling! You can't think I would fail to tell the police if I knew."

Betty thought she would.

"There's my own safety to think of, certainly," Viola added. "But listen, Betty darling. As soon as the media learn it was my place— People do remember me, so you can imagine the headlines." Betty thought she seemed rather pleased by the prospect of headlines. "I must be ready when they catch on that I'm here. . . ."

When, Betty noted. Not *if.*

"You did tell the press," Betty said accusingly.

"Not *directly*, darling. It was a terrible crime. People in New York are so clever about hearing things, and there's no stopping them." Viola got up and peered through the slats on the lowered venetian blinds. "I know too much. I blame it all on Rosellen. She can't keep her models under control."

Betty looked at Viola blankly.

"Rosellen. You *must* remember her. She's Rosellen Hamilton now." Viola tapped her toe on the carpet and sounded irritated as she said, "She went off with a husband of mine years ago, for a time. He wasn't worth keeping, so I forgave her. Then she married Henry. I knew him quite well, of course, from the old days. Rosellen was a *fabulously* successful model in the seventies, that gorgeous red hair, but you can't keep it up forever, although Lauren Hutton seems able to go on and on. . . . Rosellen and Henry have their own agency now. She always had the killer instinct, so she has the perfect job for her, wouldn't you say?" Viola seemed to think that Betty in her long tweed skirt, denim shirt, and comfortable sneakers must follow closely the ups and downs of the fashion business and its mannequins. "I should have done that myself. Things would be much easier now."

"Viola," Betty said sharply. "You are wandering." It was like hearing one of the office secretaries recount every tiny detail of last night's dream date. "Why are you here?"

Viola took a deep breath as she leaned back on Betty's sofa. "I told you I found the police at my place when I got home from visiting my very old friend for a few days, a wonderful photographer—he took that *legendary* shot of me on the Spanish Steps in Rome in the Balenciaga gown." Betty gave her a look. "I told the police that I was going to stay at the Plaza, where they could find me in the morning. Not strictly the truth, was it?" Viola grinned. "One of the detectives rather liked me, I think."

As Betty considered the implications of lying to the New York City police, Viola said brightly, "Do you have anything nice to drink? I seldom drink, only a little white wine, but this day has simply *drained* me."

Betty had a good California Chardonnay that Ted Kelso had recommended. She was planning to take it to dinner tomorrow evening. She sighed. "I'll get you something."

Viola followed her into the kitchen and kept talking while Betty uncorked the cold wine and poured a glass.

"Instead of going over to the Plaza, I got into my car and headed for the FDR Drive and Connecticut. I know it's a foolish luxury to have a car in Manhattan, but I do need to get away from the city now and then."

Betty handed her the glass and managed to herd her back into the living room. Viola grabbed the wine bottle and brought it with her.

"Viola," Betty said carefully. "Am I to understand that you told the police, who are investigating a murder in your apartment, that you would be staying at the Plaza, and here you are, many, many miles away?"

Viola beamed. "You were always so clearheaded. I get into muddles. It's hard enough looking out for oneself."

In spite of feeling mildly put upon, Betty was unable to remain cross in the face of Viola's act. "And how exactly did you find me?" she asked.

"Darling, from Rita, of course! She's been like a spiritual adviser for simply years."

"She never mentioned it to me," Betty said.

"Well, there's the confidentiality thing," Viola said solemnly. "The seal of the confessional."

Betty did not recall that the rule held for confidences between an activist nun and a childhood friend. Viola probably wasn't too strong on church doctrines, her catechism classes being far in the past, but since Sister Rita was highly principled, she would likely keep quiet if asked.

"What a lovely wine," Viola said in a tone that suggested

amazement at Betty's ability to choose an acceptable vintage. "Isn't it fun to be together again?"

Betty had never really been "together" with Viola Romanowski, being older and evidently wiser, and this wasn't exactly "fun." She said, "I must know, Viola. Is there really some danger to you from some unknown person, or is it just that the media are on your trail because of something you . . . suggest happened in New York?"

Viola smiled over the rim of her wineglass, which she had just refilled. "They are not unknown, darling, and they will be contacting me. I have told you the *absolute* truth. I'll say no more just now."

Saving it for the TV cameras? How tiresome is this going to get? Betty wondered. Then she said firmly, "In that case, perhaps we should go to bed and talk in the morning. I have some work I want to start on early."

"I thought you'd retired. Rita said you were as free as a bird. Oh, good Lord, Tina! Poor baby! I've been talking away and haven't given the precious thing a thought. I have been terribly wicked to her lately."

Betty was resigned now to the fact that Viola was completely mad.

"She's *all* alone in the car. Betty darling, if you could just slip out and fetch my bag and Tina. I simply can't risk being seen. She'll be no trouble at all."

"Who is Tina?" she asked with all the calmness she could muster. Another surprise houseguest would be too much.

"My precious kitty. She's in her traveling box. I ask you to go only because no one would ever mistake you for me."

Betty sighed. She'd had years of doing the dirty work for superiors who didn't care to put themselves in uncomfortable business situations. She supposed she could manage to fetch a bag and a precious kitty from a car parked on a dark country road some minutes after one o'clock in the morning. It seemed the only way to get Viola upstairs and into bed so she herself could get some sleep.

As Betty ventured out, she could see the shape of Viola's

car a hundred yards or so down the road. It was very quiet on Timberhill Road. Betty kept on the shoulder, close to the trees.

Suddenly she stopped and drew back into the deeper darkness of the roadside brush. She squinted into the distance. Another car was parked farther along, well off the road.

She edged along toward Viola's car, keeping as much out of sight as possible. Viola's tale of murder had stimulated her imagination. Although she knew for a certainty that it must be young lovers parked in the darkness, she couldn't help feel a little thrill of apprehension.

When she reached Viola's car—a rather plain vehicle for one who seemed to put much emphasis on glamour—she could see the large cat-carrier and a small suitcase on the backseat.

Betty hesitated before opening the door. If the overhead light came on, she would be visible to anyone who might be watching. . . .

Stop it, Elizabeth Anne, she told herself firmly. Nobody is watching.

She opened the car door and heaved out the carrying case. From its heft, it did not appear that Precious Kitty was a lightweight. She grabbed Viola's suitcase and shut the door with her hip.

It was with considerable alarm that she heard the engine of the other car come to life. No lights came on, but the sound of the engine could be clearly heard through the darkness.

Betty didn't hesitate. She raced back along the road and up the front walk to her house. As she fumbled to turn the knob with her hands full, the driver gunned the engine of the other car. Over her shoulder she saw the car make a U-turn on Timberhill Road and speed away toward the town center. The headlights had still not been turned on.

Viola was peering through the slats of the venetian blinds. She spun around when Betty dumped the overnight bag and the cat-carrying case on the living room floor. The level of the expensive Chardonnay had dropped noticeably.

"I told you so!" Viola was triumphant. "You saw them. They know where I am. " She seemed delighted to be vindicated.

"Some teenagers were making out, or whatever they call it nowadays," Betty said. But her heart was thumping.

"You'll see," Viola said. "Now, where's my darling Tina?"

She unclasped the locks of the cat box and threw back the cover.

Betty watched with sinking heart as the enormous black-and-white cat stared around the unfamiliar room with a malevolent look and then condescended to leap from the box to the floor. The cat stalked to the center of the room and sat down. It watched Betty.

"Here's your new home, Precious," Viola said. "Auntie Betty is so happy to have you here."

Wrong, Betty said to herself. To Viola she said, "Now that we're all here, I'm locking up and going to bed. We'll talk in the morning. Your room is to the right at the top of the stairs."

"Will we be safe?" Viola said. She was starting to look tired and older—or, rather, her true age.

"The car drove away, if that's what you're worried about," Betty said. "There's milk in the refrigerator if the cat wants it." She looked at the cat, who in turn was eyeing the upholstery of Betty's newish sofa as though it bore a sign reading TINA, SHARPEN YOUR CLAWS HERE.

"I brought along a lovely can of turkey bits for Tina," Viola said. "Tina loves her turkey bits, doesn't she? Almost as much as her shrimp."

Betty did not care for the idea of chatting up animals with questions that were never answered.

"Tina is a little cross," Viola said. "She doesn't like being left alone and she hates driving. I usually arrange to have her looked after when I go away, but this was different. Poor Tina was *there* when Mandi was murdered. It was

awful, wasn't it, Precious? Well! Now that we're all in the
country, we're going to forget all our troubles and have a
wonderful holiday."

Viola and Tina on a country holiday in East Moulton,
Connecticut, with Them—the press, a murderer, or both,
and quite possibly the New York City police lurking about
in the shadows. So much for the quiet days and peaceful
nights of a retired lady.

CHAPTER 8

VIOLA WENT quietly to bed, taking the dreadful Tina and the remains of the Chardonnay with her. A litter box had been contrived in the little alcove near the guest bedroom. A dish of rather distasteful-looking cat food had been placed around the corner. Even the cat seemed to find the food offensive, tiny turkey bits though it was.

Betty had put her head on her pillow with the certain knowledge that this was not going to end up a simple overnight visit, and the sense of being needed did, after all, have its limits.

And yet . . . Viola's elaborate makeup could not in the end beat back the truth of her years. Betty had seen Viola wince on climbing the stairs as though her joints rebelled against the effort. The telltale blue veins in her hands, the tiny scars around her eyes that hinted at a face-lift . . . Betty was glad not to have to struggle to sustain an impossible image to feel okay about herself.

As she closed her eyes on that thought, she had a sudden uncomfortable moment. She didn't feel all that good about herself. She was floating somewhere between her useful past life and an unclear future. She was as old as Viola, with the same aches and pains and realization that life did not go on forever.

"Stop it, Elizabeth," a more sensible part of her mind said. "Get a grip and go to sleep. You're in good shape in every way."

Betty pulled the fat, warm comforter up to her chin, but her thoughts were still on Viola. How did she live? Were her finances sufficient for this long retirement? Betty would try to ask her subtly tomorrow. She seemed to suggest that she took in guests and was paid for coaching them. Had she not saved any money from her career? Perhaps there was alimony still. Two marriages at least had been reported back in her heyday. "Foreigners," Betty's mother had sniffed, as though her parents and Betty's father's had not emigrated from the old Czechoslovakia around the First World War.

There was her tale of possible pursuit by a killer. Betty wasn't even really sure there had been a horrible murder, and she did not believe that Violetta was still a "story." What she was certain of was that if Viola had run out on the New York police, there was likely to be some bother ahead.

She drowsed. A model. What was a model? A role model, a model student. An image to emulate. A paragon, an ideal. Betty sighed. Surely not in this case.

Betty slept, but not well. She kept half waking from slumber, thinking she heard footsteps, a car stopping out front on the dark road, a door opening slowly. All nonsense, but it spoiled her rest.

Early in the morning, as the sun began to lighten the sky, Betty awoke to real footfalls, but it was only the mighty Tina squeezing through the narrow space of Viola's door which had been left ajar. Betty heard the risers on the stair creak as Tina went in search of entertainment, or, more likely, food. There was no sound from Viola's room.

Betty descended in the half light to make herself some coffee. Tina was glaring into space in the middle of the living room, but when Betty reached down to give the cat a tentative, almost friendly pat, her reward was a quick swipe of a paw that barely missed scratching her.

"So much for hospitality," Betty said. She opened the front door to a stream of cold air. "Go, enjoy the country," she said. Tina blinked. "You'll like it. Field mice and chipmunks to attack rather than your hostess. Keep off the road and lay off the birds."

The cat considered the possibilities. Slowly Tina advanced toward the open door and boldly entered the great outdoors. Betty went to the kitchen to boil water for the coffeemaker.

She was startled when the phone rang. The kitchen wall clock said six-thirty. Had the New York City police tracked the missing Viola down in her corner of East Moulton?

"Miz Trenka," the faint voice said, "it's Carole." There was a catch in Carole's voice as she whispered, "Johnny's back. I didn't know who else to call. I'm sorry it's so early, but I'm scared."

Betty thought, but not unkindly, that Carole's options-recognition skills were quite underdeveloped if the only person she could think of calling was herself. Surely there was a friend or neighbor of longer standing somewhere in East Moulton.

"It's all right," Betty said. "I was up."

Carole said slowly. "I saw him yesterday after work."

Betty really did not want to have to add Carole and her alleged husband to Viola, Tina, and Them—and yes, Crispin Abbott, her new Best Friend. On the other hand, since she'd seen Johnny the day before, she'd wondered whether he meant trouble for Carole. On the other hand, Carole had never indicated that Johnny was a threat to her.

"Where did you see him?" Betty asked, although she knew the answer.

"I was at this place about a job. . . . Never mind."

Carole seemed reluctant to explain she'd been roped in to Crispin Abbott's search for a muse to replace Sonia, only to discover Johnny Fender already established at the Winfield farm. He must not have been in touch with her. She'd once committed herself to him, only to be abandoned. How unfortunate.

"You were at the Winfield farm," Betty said when Carole failed to explain, "and discovered that Johnny is staying there."

Silence. Then Carole said, "How do you know?"

"I went to see Mr. Abbott about the typing job, and I met Johnny."

"I didn't know he was there," Carole said. "Honest. His mother works there, too. Johnny always said that property should be theirs because of some cousin."

"How did he come to be back in East Moulton, do you know?"

"He knew Mr. Abbott from before, when he was traveling around. Johnny told me once he'd met a rich man in New York who was looking for a place in Connecticut. Johnny told him about the old farm being for sale by the trustees. He said the old guy would set us up for life. Just when they started renovating the place, Johnny got into some trouble, so he left town. He promised to come back for me and Noelle, but he didn't. I didn't hear from him in all that time. So when I saw him, I freaked. I didn't know what to do, so I just left."

"Carole, I don't think you should work yourself up about this. I think you should just go about your business and do what you know is right. Don't worry until there's something to worry about. And keep away from the Winfield farm."

"Did you see it? Isn't it great? Johnny says the stuff there is worth millions." Carole took a deep breath. "I feel better now. They say you're very sensible and experienced, and they're right."

"Ah, yes. Them. You can call me if there's any trouble."

Carole sighed. "I shouldn't have bothered you, but you're like . . . like a real friend, with the typing and all. I wanted you to know in case . . . in case something happened to me." Carole hung up quickly.

Betty was thoughtful as she poured herself a cup of the really good coffee she had taken to making, and took her coffee mug to the kitchen window. Carole's anxiety could be genuine, but something disturbed Betty. Exactly why had Carole called at this impossibly early hour? Betty thought back to her days at Edwards & Son.

More than once a salesman or one of the vice presidents—or even Sid Edwards Junior—had called Sid Senior asking for advice about Situation X, but what they were really saying was "Something is going to go wrong with Situation X, and I'll be involved, but I'll escape blame because you told me what to do."

Betty had told Carole to go about her business as usual, but what Carole was saying was that she wanted to go back to Johnny, and if it was the wrong decision, Betty had told her to do what she thought was right.

Betty had found her way to the backyard, where she saw a large black-and-white mound in the middle of a patch of fading bronze chrysanthemums inherited from the previous owner. She smiled. Tina had rapidly succumbed to the joys of country living: The city cat was nibbling at some bit of formerly living country wildlife, the chipmunk that didn't get away.

When Betty went up to dress for the day, Viola was still silent behind her door. There was no sound from her when Betty descended with Crispin Abbott's manuscript under her arm and went to the small dining room, where she'd converted a corner into a makeshift office with computer and printer on a table that served as a desk and a bookcase to hold paper and other supplies. Before she started work, she made a phone call.

Officer Bob, as she called him, was the Connecticut State Police resident trooper whom she'd had occasion to meet soon after her arrival in East Moulton.

"You just caught me," he said.

Betty made it brief: What could be done for a young woman frightened by a possibly threatening husband, long absent and now back in town.

"Not much," Bob said. "What are you up to now?"

"It's the young woman who works at the East Moulton supermarket. . . ."

"Johnny Fender's wife, girlfriend, whatever. Someone said he was back in town, but he's not at his mother's house. She has some old shack up your way."

"You know about him?"

"I'd only just been assigned here last year when he came back with the girl, but his old reputation had not been forgotten by ... by the authorities, shall we say. If Carole has cause, she could probably get some judge to issue a restraining order to keep him away, for what good that would do."

"No cause yet, I'm afraid," Betty said. "She simply saw him. He's in residence at the Winfield farm, apparently as the guest of Crispin Abbott, who is widely reported to be a person of some note."

Officer Bob sighed faintly. "Johnny's a bad one. Was a bad one. They say people change." He sounded unconvinced. "I don't know anything about Abbott."

"He doesn't appear to be a criminal type," Betty said. "And he's not easy about Johnny, I suspect, who seems to do chores about the place. His mother tends to the house. Abbott's apparently quite affluent. I'm doing some typing for him."

Officer Bob said, "What I'll do is call over to the town police, tell them to keep an eye out. They've probably heard the rumors or even seen him. Some of the young guys went to high school with Johnny. I've got to run. Don't you go getting involved in somebody's domestic mess."

"No sir," she said. "Not me. But—" She stopped. She had been about to ask him about a murdered model in New York, but then she would have to explain, to mention Viola, who was certainly in some kind of trouble with the New York police for leaving town, and finally to stir up interest in something that might not even exist. Betty didn't feel like being that good a citizen so early in the morning. With luck, Viola would be gone today, anyhow, fleeing her imagined pursuers in her electric blue coat and trailing Tina behind her.

"What?" Officer Bob asked.

"Nothing," Betty said. "I forgot what it was. It's terrible to get old."

"You're not old," Bob said. "Why, I've seen you race along a road like a girl of sixteen."

"Don't remind me," Betty said. "One does amazing things to save one's skin."

She'd ask Ted Kelso about the murder later. With all those computers in his house, he could probably call up the Internet and get all the news on a New York City murder.

Betty sat down at her table and opened Crispin Abbott's fat envelope. If she read it straight through now, before she started typing, she'd be able to respond in some noncommittal way when Abbott called her. She had no doubt that he would not wait for her to call him.

At one point the word "mannequin" caught her eye. She paused to read the paragraph more closely, but it was nothing about Violetta. That would have been too much. The woman was nameless (how gentlemanly), "a voluptuous titan-haired wench who stole my heart and my money for a brief and memorable week, and who was promptly stolen away by a man she'd stolen away from a woman who had in turn stolen him from his wife. I recall this incident only because the next week I married my third wife and began six years of perfect hell with an undeniably crazed person in my bed, and, worse, at my breakfast table. . . ."

Poor Crispin Abbott. A genius perpetually unlucky in love and willing to talk about it.

After a time she went to look out the kitchen window for Tina, but Tina was not to be seen. Betty hoped that chipmunk or field mouse à la carte was tastier than store-bought turkey bits.

It was going to start out as another clear day, but a band of gray clouds on the horizon promised rain later. For the moment the rising sun was making the remaining leaves glow red and gold.

Suddenly Betty caught a glimpse of movement behind the fringe of evergreens and shrubs along the side of her unusable garage. She squinted through her thick glasses. The dark tree trunks and drooping pine branches seemed to form themselves into the shape of a person. Tallish, definitely not one of the three Whitey Saks boys.

"Hello!" Betty called out boldly. "Is there something you want?"

The movement behind the branches stopped, and Betty wondered if she'd imagined it.

All at once Tina bolted from the undergrowth around the evergreens where Betty had seen the movement. The cat barreled toward the house at a speed surprising for a creature of that size. Tina was up the steps and past in what seemed like a second. Betty frowned. Had she seen something, or had the considerable weight of Tina blundering around the trees merely set up a chain reaction of movement?

There was nothing to be seen now.

Tina, exhausted by her country holiday, had staked out a spot on the little area rug near the stairs to the second floor, but Betty was not about to attempt friendliness again in the face of Tina's manifest hostility.

There was still no sound from the guest room above when Betty listened at the foot of the stairs. Violetta continued to sleep the sleep of the discriminating drinker of decent California Chardonnay.

Her phone rang again.

"Elizabeth," Ted Kelso said, "are you aware that someone with cameras, including a video camera, is parked on the street in front of your house, taking pictures? What have you been up to while I was away?"

Oh, Viola, Betty thought. "I was unaware," she said to Ted. "I haven't been up to anything, but . . ." She hesitated. "If I ask you to find some information for me about something that happened in New York yesterday or the day before, will you refrain from asking questions right now?"

"Of course," Ted said promptly.

"It was a crime," Betty said. "A young woman was murdered in New York City. I understand she was a model, and I think her name was Mandi."

"Mmm," Ted said. "Murder." Betty could imagine him

stroking his short gray beard and shaking his head over the latest folly of his near neighbor, Elizabeth Anne Trenka.

Betty sighed. "I have a visitor. A childhood friend named Viola Romanowski. She used to be a model—a rather famous one. She called herself Violetta back then."

"Is *she* still alive?" Ted said. "That's stupid. Of course she is. Is she somehow connected to the murdered girl and the photographer?"

"I wish I could say no," Betty said, "but she is. But not," she added hastily, "as the murderer." She had a moment of deep anxiety. If Viola actually had murdered someone, Betty was harboring a criminal. The anxiety passed quickly. She'd claim ignorance, citing Viola's lifelong habit of making up good stories. "What should I do about this photographer?"

"Send him packing," Ted said. "I have no doubt you can handle that."

Betty thought for a moment. "Yes," she said, "I can. If the person cites a reason for being here, I shall provide a better reason for being elsewhere, bothering someone else."

"I'm looking forward to hearing tonight about your meeting with the legendary Crispin Abbott," Ted said.

"I was hired," Betty said. "For the moment. I rather like him."

It was barely a minute after she hung up with Ted that Penny Saks called.

"I don't want to alarm you," Penny said, sounding quite alarmed, "but there is a woman with a camera prowling around at the back of your house, and a man in front of your house next to a car, and there's this other car I don't recognize parked down the street. I saw them when I took the boys out for the school bus." She stopped for breath.

"I'll handle it," Betty said firmly. "It is not a problem."

"That's a relief," Penny said. The longish pause indicated that she was desperate to know more.

Betty thought quickly. "I'm doing some confidential work for that famous person at the Winfield farm," she said. "I can't tell you more right now, but it seems the press has gotten wind of it. You know how they are. Please say nothing."

"Not a word," Penny said. She was thrilled.

Having promised Penny she'd tell all when she was able, Betty went out to the shabby blue car parked beside her mailbox. It was surely the same one she'd seen passing yesterday. That gave her pause. If this was the media after Viola in the wake of the murder, then the media had known that Viola would be here well before she'd arrived late last night.

"Can I be of assistance?" Betty said in the tone she had often used to address representatives of companies that called on Edwards & Son and tried to sell overpriced fax paper to new receptionists.

The lumpish man in a trench coat quickly tried to conceal his video camera behind him. A still camera with a long lens hung on a cord around his neck.

"No," the man said. Betty peered into the car. The front seat was littered with paper cups and McDonald's bags.

"I think you have been given the wrong information about this house," Betty said. "There is nothing here worth photographing." She glanced at him sternly through her thick glasses.

"My information is good," he said defensively. He looked her over as though he might have some doubts that this tall woman in a denim shirt, long skirt, and sensible low-heeled shoes could be anybody he was supposed to get pictures of.

"You and your colleague who is trespassing out back," Betty said, "should know that I have called the resident state trooper."

"We're not breaking any laws."

"She, at least, is trespassing. I think," Betty went on, "that you would do better to lurk about the estate of Crispin Abbott. He is quite well known, and would probably welcome your attention. He lives a mile or two along this road. New mailbox at the roadside. Whoever sent you doubtless knows all about him."

"Crispin Abbott? Didn't he just get sued?"

"Many lawsuits," Betty said cheerfully. "Many scandals. Many wives and lovers. Everyone in New York knows him. And if you are looking for Violetta, as I assume you are, you should know that she is his guest at the Winfield farm, not mine."

"True?" The photographer looked at Betty with narrowed eyes, trying to read the truth. "How'd you know we're looking for her? They said she'd be here."

"My good man, this is a small town, everyone knows everything. I did know her a long time ago, but this"—she gestured toward her small house—"this is scarcely what the great Violetta would find comfortable." She prayed that Viola would remain safely asleep until after these intruders had gone.

"How far did you say to the Abbott place?" He opened the door of his car.

"Can't be more than a mile. And please take your colleague with you. I am a busy woman. I can't have this nonsense going on."

"We'll be back, you know, if I don't find her." The man started the engine and began to move off down Timberhill Road.

"Hey!" An athletic young woman with cameras slung around her shoulders ran from behind Betty's house and sprinted after the blue car. It came to a stop a hundred yards away, and the young woman opened the passenger side door.

"Watch out for the dogs," Betty called after them. "Those Rhodesian ridgebacks are very protective of their territory. Have a nice day."

Betty marched back into her house. Viola had now slept just about long enough.

CHAPTER 9

EARLY IN the morning, while Violetta slept and Tina frolicked in Connecticut, the two New York City homicide detectives drank bad coffee in a Greek coffee shop on the corner of an East Side cross street and Third Avenue, and pondered what to do about Viola Roman. Danny Nealon and Fred Carver had been somewhat disturbed to discover that among the missing was Viola Roman, aka Viola Romanowski, aka Viola Las Palmas (long ago and briefly), aka Viola Ardmore (briefly, and more recently), and aka simply Violetta, with the portfolio to prove it.

She had never checked in at the Plaza, not under the various names acquired through her profession and marriages. If their description of her to the Plaza staff was any good at all, she hadn't checked in under any other name either.

"I hope we never find her," Fred said grumpily. "She's nuts. Even if she did it, she'll get off. 'Something snapped, your honor. . . .' "

"She's not crazy. She conned us, and we have to find her," Danny Nealon said.

"We got those leads about the boyfriends. That's good for now."

"Not good enough," Danny said stubbornly. "The Hamilton woman at the agency can maybe help us. Viola doesn't like her. And Viola never got around to giving us the name of the friend in New Jersey she was visiting, which isn't very cooperative. Well, I'm ahead of her on that one."

Fred said, "She definitely sounded off to me. Who is this

'they' she kept talking about? Mob guys? Green men from Mars?"

Danny Nealon said, "The way I see it, she used to be famous. Remember those pictures in the apartment? She was a pretty big model twenty-five, thirty years ago, then suddenly it's all over. One day she had the high life—money, clothes, drugs, playboys and millionaires after her, the old entourage wherever she went. She was beautiful, rich, she's had the world at her feet, and bam! Overnight comes the first wrinkle and she's dead meat. She loses it all. Know what I mean?"

"Yeah," Fred said, and looked doubtful.

"What I'm saying, Fred, is Viola lost it all. For years she muddles along, taking in paying guests and doing this and that to survive. Then suddenly this Mandi is dead in her apartment, and she's got a chance to be somebody again for a couple of minutes. She says the murderer is after her, and she'll be in all the papers. Bingo! Violetta isn't gone, she's right there on the front page. She's a celebrity again, the way she was when she was young and beautiful."

"She'd be an even bigger story if she were the murderer," Fred said glumly. "How do you know all this stuff about her?"

Danny shrugged and finished his coffee. "Guy from my old neighborhood used to be a stringer for some gossip columnist. He knows about these people. I called him last night. He didn't know zip about Mandi, she was too new on the scene. He knew about Violetta though. She was pretty wild in the old days, but nothing that would indicate she'd murder a comparative stranger. As far as he knew, she never murdered anyone in the old days either, but . . ."

Fred finished the thought for Danny. "But she might know who did do it, and that could put her in danger, so she ran. I suppose we do have to find her."

"I've got those names and addresses from her desk at the apartment. We can start calling people to see if she's hiding out with any of them," Danny said. "After we see Rosellen Hamilton at the model agency."

* * *

If Violetta had managed to hang on to her allure from the old days, Rosellen Hamilton was still pretty much in full bloom, and she was definitely larger than life. She seemed to tower over the two detectives, and in spite of appearing willowy, she was not scrawny. In this she was in sharp contrast to the skinny girls in jeans and baggy shirts the two men had seen sitting about the reception area, clutching huge leather portfolios and looking like orphans. Indeed, it took a close look to see that the girls were really very beautiful, but were hiding it behind semi-grunge camouflage.

"Mandi was promising," Rosellen said condescendingly as she swept them into her office. The white walls were covered with gigantic blow-ups of Rosellen's face, full and in profile. No doubt who was the boss here. She strode ahead of the two men. In a dark-green jacket with a vaguely military look, short dark curly hair with reddish highlights, chunky gold earrings, pale luminous skin, and dramatic dark brows over greenish eyes, she was an impressive figure. She sat gracefully in a padded black leather chair behind her desk and indicated that the detectives should sit in the two chairs facing her.

"Only promising?" Danny said. He knew she was in her forties and had had her days of modeling fame fifteen years before, but she was still actively glamorous, whereas Viola Roman was more an echo of glamour.

Rosellen leaned forward, businesslike. "She'd been with us for a few months. Her booker, Alison, can tell you exactly how long. It takes time for a girl to build. She was responsible enough about going to her go-sees. She showed up on time when she had a booking. The clients liked her, but she hadn't hit it big. We had some catalog work lined up for her last week, but she missed those appointments. Now we know why, don't we? The clients don't care what the excuse is, however, so she lost us some money. Not much. We made adjustments." She managed a surreptitious look at the thin, expensive watch on her wrist. She was wearing a narrow wedding band on her left hand, and on the middle finger of her right hand a wide, heavy gold ring with a silver lion medallion in the center. She tapped the pale, polished nail of the finger with the ring on the desk impatiently.

"Drugs? Problems with men?"

Rosellen was suddenly wary. "Not as far as I know." The nail tapped again. "You'd have to talk to Alison. Some girls get close to their bookers. She was new to New York, she couldn't have known many people. She . . ." Tap, tap went the fingernail.

"You hesitated," Danny said. Out of the corner of his eye he could see that Fred wasn't about to open his mouth.

"I don't pry into the private lives of my girls as long as they do their jobs. I certainly had no interest in Mandi Webb's tangled affairs."

"You didn't like Mandi," Danny said.

Rosellen looked at him steadily. "I suppose not. I did not find her likeable. A schemer. But an amateur schemer."

"Mmm. What can you tell us about her relationship with Viola Roman? How they met and so forth."

Rosellen's expression was unreadable. "Poor Violetta," she finally said, and leaned back in her chair. "Another schemer. The queen of schemers. It was Viola who brought Mandi in to see me originally. I don't know how they hooked up, but Viola does advertise a room to rent in that cluttered little apartment of hers. She shuddered elegantly. "The cat is dreadful. I'm amazed anyone would want to stay." Rosellen suddenly opened her eyes wide in a practiced expression of wonder and surprise. "Did *Viola* murder Mandi? Is that why you're asking these questions? Of course! I should have seen it! We all know Viola is mad— and for some reason something snapped and Viola crushed the life out of that poor child."

Danny and Fred exchanged glances, and Danny went on smoothly. "Did you socialize?"

"With Mandi? Heavens no!"

"I meant Viola Roman. You were both in the business."

"She is much older, from a generation of models that preceded mine. We had little in common."

"You must have acquaintances in common. She talked about enemies, old secrets. She claims she has enemies, that the murderer was after her."

Rosellen smiled a little. "Gentlemen, naturally she'd say that if she had committed the murder. Remember, she's crafty. She's had to be. She never thought much about the future, what she'd do when nobody wanted her look anymore and she got too old for the camera. She must have put some money away, but not enough. Whatever she's claiming now . . ." Rosellen's gesture took in her office. "I had a plan. Always. I can afford to be kind, and I've done her favors from time to time, sending her girls who need a place to stay for a few weeks until their money starts coming in." Rosellen sat up, a signal perhaps that her patience with the interview had reached an end. "Viola has made enemies over the years. I said she was a schemer. Perhaps worse."

"Reason we're asking," Danny said, "is we have information that she was once married to somebody who dumped her for you."

Rosellen took her time in answering, but the fingernail tapped on the desk again. "Pat Ardmore," she said. "Yes. Everybody knows that. I'm not especially proud of that episode, but I was young and foolish, and Viola was getting on. She must have been at least thirty-five. It was nothing really. I haven't seen him for years, and neither has Viola, I'm sure. He lives abroad, and I've been happily married for a long time to someone else. Does this have anything to do with Mandi's murder?"

Danny shrugged. "We don't know. Hamilton's your married name?"

"Yes," she said shortly.

"Mr. Hamilton, your husband. Is he involved in your business?"

"A bit. He looks after the financial side. I handle the creative side."

"But he would know Viola Roman."

"Certainly they've met," she said. "We have a couple of

big parties every year at our weekend place in Litchfield, up in Connecticut. She came to one or two."

"Thank you, Mrs. Hamilton," Danny said. He got up and Fred jumped to his feet. "You wouldn't know where Viola is now."

Rosellen frowned. "Now?"

"She seems to have left town. If you hear from her . . ."

"Why would I hear from her?" Rosellen betrayed a certain anxiety about the prospect.

"We ought to talk to Alison now," Danny said.

Rosellen relaxed perceptibly as she stood. "You can use the conference room. Alison will join you when she's off the phone."

At the door, Danny paused. "Mrs. Hamilton, do you know any of these people?" He fished a handwritten list from his pocket. "Corin Williams. Nell Cross. Betty Trenka. Sandra Krell. Rita Hayek."

Rosellen frowned. "Corin was a very well-known fashion photographer in the old days. He's retired now, and lives in New Jersey, I believe. Someone told me his mind . . . wanders a bit. Nell and Sandra were two of my girls who stayed with Viola for a while. They've both left the business. What were the other names? No, I don't recognize them. It is important?"

"Maybe," Danny said. "Ah, there's one more. Henry Hamilton. Would that be your husband?"

"Yes."

Danny thought it was interesting how a beautiful woman like Rosellen Hamilton could suddenly look pinched and old. "Is Mr. Hamilton available to speak with us?" he asked.

"He's away on business," Rosellen said sharply. "He's been on the West Coast for several days. He'd have nothing to add to what I've told you, I'm sure. He didn't know Mandi."

"Have him call us when he gets back." Fred spoke for the first time, perhaps given voice by the fact they were leaving the intimidating Rosellen.

The conference room was small but very comfortable.

The two men sat side by side at the long table, and the receptionist brought them coffee.

"Where'd you come up with those names?" Fred was still grumpy. "You never mentioned Henry Hamilton to me."

"I picked up the names from the desk, and around the apartment. I found Hamilton's business card on the floor. The two girls had sent Christmas cards to Viola. Rita Hayek seems to be an old friend, maybe a relative. Corin Williams is a little out of it. He's got to be her friend in New Jersey. When I called, he swore he'd just seen Viola, but then he started talking as though they'd been on some fashion shoot in Europe and had run into Christian Dior on the street."

"Maybe they did," Fred said.

"Dior died years ago. I checked. The other woman's name, Betty Trenka, and a Connecticut phone number were jotted down on the back of a cash register receipt from a supermarket two blocks from the Roman apartment. I called the number, but there was no answer. We'll try her later. There's another thing I haven't told you. . . . I'll tell you later," Danny said as a plump, bouncy young woman in jeans burst into the room. She was the complete antithesis of the waifish models and hopeful waifs in the reception area.

"Hi! I'm Alison. You wanted to talk to me?"

"Yes," Danny said. "We're gathering information about Mandi Webb."

Alison shook her head. "What a lousy thing to happen. She was okay, you know? Not real smart, if you know what I mean, but she would have done all right in the business. Maybe not million-dollar cosmetic contracts, but she was learning fast."

"Was she likable?"

Alison shrugged. "Likable? She was a kid from the sticks. Everybody from out there starts out nice and pretty. Something in the water, you think? It's when they're here for a while that they change."

"Boyfriends?" Fred asked.

"She was seeing a couple of guys, I think. She just came out of the wilderness, for gosh sakes. Why not enjoy it?"

"Know their names?"

Alison shook her head. "She kept her mouth shut. She used to hang out at some places the models and the young social types go, and the sports types and the show-biz types and the rich old men looking for young things, but Mandi was sensible enough. If you're starting out, you can't stay up too late if you want to look great at eight in the morning for the camera." She thought for a minute. "Mandi was staying with Viola Roman. She might know. She used to be—"

Both Danny and Fred raised a hand to stop the explanation.

"We know," Danny said. "Do you know Viola Roman?"

"Personally? I've seen her only when she drops in here."

"Often?"

"Pretty often. She still looks great. Rumor is that Henry advises her on her investments. They say he's good with money."

"That's Mr. Hamilton, I take it? Okay, about Mandi's boyfriends. Viola claims to have no idea who Mandi's boyfriends were. Mrs. Hamilton says the same."

Alison shrugged. "Rosie wouldn't. She saves her deep, abiding interest for the big names who bring in the big bucks." Then she hesitated. "I don't want to get anybody in trouble, but Mandi did mention a guy who sounded real interested in her. Not too long ago either." Alison looked briefly troubled. "No name or anything, but he sounded too good to be true, so I warned her to be careful. Like, he could afford all the nice things these kids want. It could have been some rock-music maniac from California for all I know, and there's no telling what they're capable of, but I got the impression that he wasn't in show business, but he knew his way around New York. Best I can do." She stopped. "She did say once he'd marry her, but he couldn't afford a divorce. Maybe she pressed him too hard."

"If we could have a list of her appointments for the last few weeks," Danny said.

"Fellas! You want to ruin our business? You want Bloomingdale's on your case? Donna Karan? Calvin *Klein* for heaven's sake? These people don't care a thing about the models. They're just a body and a face who'd better show up on time and do the job. Besides, Mandi was so new to the business, she didn't have any leverage."

"We'll be discreet," Danny said. "We may not need to follow up."

Alison shrugged again. "I'll leave it with the receptionist, but don't screw up, okay? Henry will have my head if you do, and then it will get back to Rosie. He and Rosie are some team. They're competing right up there with Elite and the Fords and Wilhelmina."

"We understand he's been away."

Alison opened her mouth, then closed it again and frowned. "Must be," she said. "I haven't seen him lately."

"Does he have much to do with the models?"

"Fellas, I don't know anything about Henry Hamilton's business. He signs my paycheck, and he's not about to get tight with me with all these gorgeous young things around, so I can't tell you anything."

Alison quickly went back to her bank of phones.

Danny and Fred departed the brick Federal-style town house that housed Rosellen's agency.

"Nothing," Fred said. The sky was clouded over and a sharp, cold wind came swirling along the street from the not-too-distant East River.

Danny said, "Maybe there's something. People in this case know things they're not saying." He was looking at the Connecticut number jotted down on the back of the grocery receipt.

"Maybe it was one of these stalkers?" Fred asked hopefully. Then he shook his head. "Wishful thinking. Those guys tend to knock on the door and blow their beloved away after they don't get answers to their letters. Or maybe Viola got upset because her paying guest was going to move out, marry that guy."

Danny wasn't paying much attention. He was looking at

a slip of white paper. "Listen, Fred, this is what I was going to tell you." He held out a grocery store receipt. "From the apartment. What do you see?"

Fred looked at both sides carefully. "Uh-oh," he said. "This receipt is dated the day before yesterday. Viola said she'd been away for a week. The girl had been dead three days when they found her. Three grocery items, taxable, at fifty-five cents each. Fish, seventy-five cents. What the hell kind of fish can you buy for seventy-five cents? A square inch of salmon? One clam? My wife says the price of fish in this city is out of sight."

"There's something I want to check," Danny said. "I think there's a supermarket over on the next avenue."

Fred waited outside the supermarket while Danny went inside. He was back in five minutes with a plastic bag in one hand and a cash register receipt in the other.

"Take a look, Freddie."

"Groceries taxable, fifty-nine cents; fish, fifty cents."

"You can buy two shrimp for fifty cents," Danny said. "Plus one can of cat food, groceries taxable. Viola said it right out to that damned cat. Shrimp. Nobody's going to like that cat enough to feed it shrimp except its owner. What it says is she was right here in New York at nine-thirty at night according to the time on her receipt, two days ago—two days after Mandi was murdered—buying shrimp for her cat. Feeding her cat while Mandi was lying dead in the bedroom, and then she was gone again until she turned up when we were there."

"She killed Mandi?" Fred asked, but it was only half a question.

"Or else she came home and found the body and left. Or she saw the murderer. Or she knew who did it. And the window. Remember it was open? She wouldn't have left it open because of the cat, so maybe somebody else was there after the murder and after Viola. Freddie, maybe 'they' are looking for her after all."

CHAPTER 10

BETTY STOOD outside Viola's door and knocked.

"Viola, wake up. We have to talk. It's important."

She heard a murmur behind the door. It was already after ten. Time enough for Viola to be up and explaining how the photographers had found Betty's house and were looking for Violetta.

Finally Viola spoke through the door. "Darling, it takes me ages to get my face together. I can't be seen by—"

"The photographers have gone, for the moment," Betty said.

"I *knew* I could count on the press to remember me! But where have they gone?"

"I sent them off to harass a man named Crispin Abbott who lives farther along Timberhill Road."

Viola was silent for a moment. "Crispin Abbott? Why, darling, I *know* him! From years and years ago. What a delightful man, terribly ugly, but he always had a gorgeous woman on his arm. A wonderfully scandalous life. How divine that Crispin is right here in this very town. But how do you know him?"

"I'm typing his autobiography. It's confidential."

"That *must* be a treat. I'd love to know all the dirty details. But, Betty, why did you send my photographers away?"

"So you could avoid them," Betty said.

"Why would I want to do that?" Viola sounded totally mystified. "Never mind. They'll be back. It will give me time to look decent. You might not understand, but it's important to me financially. Things have not been easy."

Betty said, "I think I do understand, but I am not happy about it. And, Viola, you must call the New York police to tell them where you are. I'm going to drive into town now. I have some business at the bank." She was going to deposit Crispin Abbott's check before he stopped payment for sending the press after him. Or perhaps he, like Viola, would welcome the attention, and Betty would receive a bonus. "When I return, you will be up and ready to talk." Then she added hopefully, "Before you go on your way . . ."

"Betty, dear, dear Betty. I told you a *tiny* untruth," Viola said, and Betty listened with a sinking heart. Viola opened the bedroom door a crack, but not enough to expose her makeup-less face, her tousled hair, and (heaven help us) her wrinkles. "I can't leave for a day or two. Someone who owes me a *great* deal is coming here to give me something." She whispered, although there was no one but Betty to hear, "It's another financial matter, and it's even more important than the press thing. My future depends on it. I couldn't arrange it in New York since the police were hanging about because of Mandi."

"Everything is important, it seems," Betty said. Her irritation was increasing. "We'll talk about it when I get back." Betty started down the stairs. The short drive to Main Street might put her in a better mood to deal with Viola.

"As long as you're going to be in town," Viola called after her. "Please, please stop at that supermarket and pick up more cat food. I've used up what I had. Turkey or liver is good. And poor Tina hasn't had a nibble of fresh shrimp in over two days."

"Shrimp for cats is beyond my means," Betty said. And beyond the bounds of common sense, she thought, most certainly for felines who respond to a gentle touch with a whack of the paw.

"I may get a call." Viola's last words reached Betty as she opened the front door. She wondered if the strange call yesterday could have been the one Viola awaited, albeit some hours too early.

Betty actually did calm down in the course of her drive, except she couldn't remember whether Tina had been left in the house or outdoors. She hoped Precious Kitty could manage to fend for herself until she returned.

After depositing Crispin Abbott's check at her bank, she pulled into the supermarket lot. She didn't care all that much about Tina's food needs, but she could learn how Carole was faring in the face of Johnny's return to the town.

"Where's Carole?" she asked the man at the register. He was retired and worked part-time stocking the shelves, helping out at the second register only when there was a rush.

"She didn't come in," the man said. "Ask the manager." He jerked his head toward the glass booth that served as the office.

The manager was a scrawny, perpetually weary man with thinning hair and a taste for narrow ties and rolled-up sleeves. He chose resentment over concern. Betty had seen a lot like him in her years in the business world. "She screwed up good this time," he said sourly. "She called in sick."

"How odd," Betty said. "I spoke to her quite early this morning, and she said nothing about being ill or not coming to work. Did you take the call?"

"The bookkeeper did. Good thing I didn't. I would have fired her on the spot. I tell you what I hear," the manager said. "I hear she runs around till all hours of the night, drinking and carousing with guys from out of town, leaving her kid home alone. No wonder she can't make it in to work."

"I wonder who's saying that?" Betty said.

"Everybody. You should hear Beatrice Fender on the subject, and she should know. She's one of my oldest customers."

That, Betty supposed, guaranteed the absolute truth.

The manager offered a parting shot. "Bea Fender won't even shop here when Carole's working. She told me so herself not an hour ago. I can't have a girl here who drives away my best customers."

Betty didn't care to get into a discussion on that matter, but she noted the fact that Bea had been shopping at the supermarket that morning, so she must have known that Carole wasn't going to be there. She said, "Do you have Carole's number?"

"Yeah, but you're not going to get her. I tried calling her myself. No answer. Sick, my foot."

After she'd bought cat food and cat litter, Betty used the pay phone outside the store to call Carole. She'd never been to her house, but she knew it was in a section of East Moulton that might be called the wrong side of the tracks, had there been any tracks running through the town. There was no answer.

She kept a little photocopied map of the town in the glove compartment. With its help, she traced a route to the cluster of streets where Carole lived about a half a mile in the other direction from the center of East Moulton.

She turned off Main Street onto a bumpy street lined with small, undistinguished shingle an clapboard houses with ragged lawns. Here and there were a few big but neglected old houses left over from the days of the large families that small-town people seemed to produce. No one was in sight in late morning.

The road curved and Betty found herself passing even more unkempt lawns and shabby houses. Finally she stopped at random at a white house with a sagging porch, got out, and went to the door. There was no doorbell, so Betty knocked firmly several times.

Eventually a bleary-eyed woman in a flowered housecoat answered and peered suspiciously at Betty through the glass of the storm door.

"I don't want whatever you're selling," she said. "Go away."

"I'm looking for Carole Fender's house," Betty said. "She works at the supermarket. Is it around here?"

"Her," the woman sniffed. "Fender is only what she calls herself. I know Beatrice Fender for years, and you should hear what she calls her." Then the woman relented. "Two houses down, a yellow place. But she's not home. I saw her driving away early this morning in that old heap of hers."

"Alone?"

"Now, how would I know that? I don't keep track of the people in the neighborhood." The woman had had enough of Betty. She slammed the door, leaving Betty to stare at her reflection in the glass of the storm door.

Betty found the house. It was set back from the street, and one big old oak still stood out front. A child's tricycle was tipped over on the grass, and the narrow porch boasted an old-fashioned glider. Betty knocked, and then peered in through the windows that looked out onto the porch. Behind the thin white curtains she saw only an empty living room, neat and not fancy.

She tore a page from the notepad she always carried and wrote "Please call me as soon as you come home," signed it, and included her phone number. Then she thought for a second. Carole said she often left little Noelle with a neighbor. The house to the left looked empty, with uncurtained windows and the grass a long-unmowed tangle. The house on the other side appeared to be occupied, but no one answered the doorbell.

At the house across the street, however, she heard a child crying. After a delay, she managed to summon a young and very pregnant woman to the door.

"Yeah, I take care of Carole's kid sometimes. She pays me," she added defensively. "I had to keep Noelle last night until nine, when Carole finally came and got her."

"Did you see anyone at Carole's house last night or this morning?"

The young woman, whose name turned out to be Sharon, looked uncomfortable. "Well, yeah. Somebody was over there last night for a little while. I saw the headlights when he left. Carole is dating a couple guys, but I don't know nothing. She left for work early today just like always right after Noelle got picked up by the school bus for preschool."

"Do you know Johnny Fender?"

"Oh, yeah. He was a big kid in high school when I was still in grammar school. Really good-looking, those eyes and that build, but my mom would have killed me if I even said hi to him. They say the cops ran him out of town right after he came back with Carole. She was always saying he'd come back for her, but I told her she was better off without him."

"That bad?" Betty murmured.

Sharon shook her head. "He was always in trouble. They say he straightened out after he went away and came back with Carole last spring. Noelle's her kid, you know, not his. My mom said she tricked him, not saying anything about Noelle until after, but I don't think that's so."

"Johnny is back in town. Could it have been him at Carole's place last night?"

Sharon became stony-faced. "I don't know nothing," she repeated.

"But you like Carole?" Betty wanted her to say yes just to confirm her own feeling that Carole wasn't as bad as she'd been painted.

"Well ... she's okay. I don't have any problems with her. She's a little stuck up, like East Moulton isn't worth her time, and she's talked about leaving when something she's been waiting for comes through." Sharon looked over her shoulder. The child had stopped crying, but the television set was on. "It's almost time for my soaps," she said. "I got to go."

"Here's my number," Betty said. "Call me if you think there's any problem."

"What kind of problem?"

"I don't know," Betty said. "I expect you'll recognize it when you see it."

Sharon promised to call. Betty had to be satisfied with that.

On her way home, driving along Main Street, Betty thought about what Sharon had said: Carole was expecting something to happen so she could leave. Not unlike Viola. Expectations in East Moulton were running high.

The Perkins pharmacy was just up ahead, and Betty pulled into an open parking space in front. She'd pick up some unnecessary odds and ends, and ask Molly casually if she had seen Carole around town. Then she'd leave quickly. The comings and goings of customers with gossip to share made it easier to slip away from Molly in the pharmacy than on the street.

"Why, Betty, you just have to think of a person and lo and behold . . ." Molly was effusively delighted to see her. "You'll never guess."

"No," Betty said. "I never will."

"Not half an hour ago someone was in asking about the Elizabeth Trenka place."

"Who?" Betty was deeply curious. More press?

"A man, nice-looking. Didn't give his name, of course. City dress, I'd say."

"Did he indicate why he was looking for me?"

"Now, I didn't say that. He asked about your *house*."

Viola again, surely. Maybe it was the person she was waiting for.

"I was going to call and warn you," Molly said, and looked expectantly at Betty in the hope of an explanation. "Then we got busy, so I didn't have the chance."

"I don't know that I need warning," Betty said.

"Connecticut plates on his car."

"Indeed. Then perhaps it was someone I used to work with in Hartford who happened to be in this part of the state." She didn't believe that, however. Nobody from the old days ever called her Elizabeth.

"You're getting more aspirin?" Molly asked. "Headaches bothering you?"

"More like old bones," Betty said. "Have you seen Carole today? She didn't go to work because she was sick, so I thought she might have stopped here to pick up something for what was ailing her."

Molly pursed her lips in disapproval. "She wasn't in. She must be playing hooky. She's got that little girl to take care of, but she's got no sense of responsibility if you ask me."

"Now, you don't know that."

"Bea Fender says—"

"I hear she's working at the Winfield farm," Betty said.

Molly said briskly, "It's not permanent, I understand. She's talking about moving to Florida. She's expecting some money, although Perk says it's too late to claim anything from the Winfield estate. The old farm sold for a lot, but Bea was only a third cousin, and there were other cousins closer. I don't understand that kind of business. That Bea and Johnny were always a pair. Bea can hold a grudge forever, and Johnny used to tear up this town something awful. Oh-oh, Perk's calling me from the back." She started away.

"Molly," Betty called after her. "You do know that Johnny's back in town."

"Lord, let's hope not," Molly said, and disappeared into her husband's sanctum.

Betty went home with her bag of tiny cans of excessively expensive cat food and a bag of litter for the cat box. Tina was sitting in the living room, staring at the front door.

Viola was not yet downstairs.

"Animal organs in gravy," Betty said to the cat. "Come and get it."

Tina actually seemed quite pleased to see Betty and rubbed against her leg as the dish was placed on the floor. Food was clearly the one true path to the cat's good graces.

She'd give Viola a few more minutes. In the meantime, she went to her makeshift office to work for a bit on Crispin's manuscript. The pile of yellow lined pages were still where she had left them, but it seemed to her that the manuscript had been disturbed. Had Viola come downstairs and

taken a peek at Crispin's scandalous life according to him?
It would be like her.

She brought up her word processing program and typed
CHAPTER ONE.

"I was born and raised in a small town eight miles from
the top of the Alleghenies . . ."

Betty typed carefully, as though she were the new girl in
the typing pool, worried that she'd make mistakes and have
to correct the six carbons.

CHAPTER 11

AT QUARTER to twelve Betty tried calling Carole again, but again no one answered. Then she dialed Crispin Abbott's number as she had promised. Although she really had nothing to say about his manuscript, she thought she could manage some soothing words so that he would not feel obliged to call her constantly. The number rang busy.

At noon Betty decided that no one—not even Viola—needed that much time to make herself look presentable for the cameras. She ascended to the second floor and knocked on the guest room door.

There was no reply. She opened the door, and discovered that Viola was no longer asleep in the little house on Timberhill Road.

Her belongings were scattered about the guest bedroom, and a clutter of makeup bottles, brushes, and tubes filled the little shelf under the medicine cabinet mirror in the bathroom. From the upstairs windows Viola was not visible outside at the back of the house. From the front Betty saw that her car was still parked on the shoulder of Timberhill Road.

Betty stood in her living room and frowned. Options: Viola had gone for a walk along Timberhill Road. She could have crossed the field to Penny Saks's house, although it was hard to imagine why. She might have ventured across the street to Ted Kelso's house, but Betty thought Ted would not tolerate her presence for more than the few seconds it would take to open and close his front door. She might even have set out across the fields behind Betty's

house, a trek that would eventually bring her to the
Winfield farm—but she didn't believe Viola was up for a
hike of that distance.

She pondered the elements of the situation: The man
who asked Molly about the way to Betty's house. The photographers who'd been told in advance of Viola's presence.
The "somebody" who was bringing something important to
Viola. The New York police. The murderer.

Quickly, Betty went back upstairs. Viola's bright blue
coat was not in the guest room closet or anywhere in the
room. Her high-heeled shoes were not in evidence, nor
were the little black dress and pearls she'd been wearing
last night. Downstairs, Betty didn't find the coat in the tiny
foyer closet. At least Viola hadn't been dragged from the
house in her nightgown.

Betty sat in her kitchen. Tina wandered in and mewed
wistfully, indicating a definite change of heart about Betty.
"Hush," Betty said. "I'm thinking . . ." She caught herself.
She was talking to a cat. That had to stop.

The first thing to do was to call the neighbors.

There was no answer at the Saks house, but Ted Kelso
answered immediately.

"I would have been astonished to see the creature you
describe on my doorstep," he said, "and after thirty seconds
of viewing the legendary Violetta I would surely have
turned her away. No, she is not here. But," he said, "I do
have confirmation of the murder of a young woman in New
York City. Found strangled yesterday, probably murdered
four days ago. An aspiring model named Mandi Webb."

"That's her," Betty said. That much of Viola's story was
true.

"And the photographers?" Ted asked.

"Viola apparently arranged for them to come here. I sent
them off to bother Crispin Abbott, although they'll have a
hard time getting over his chain-link fence if he doesn't
want to see them."

"Did you mention Abbott to your missing houseguest?"

"Actually I did," Betty said. "She said she'd met him in the old days."

"Then that's where she's gone. People famous in reality or just in their own minds like to club together."

"Then she must have walked there, because her car is still out on the road," Betty said, "but that's pretty hard to imagine if you know Viola."

"She'll turn up," Ted said. "Maybe the photographers scooped her up. Dinner is on for seven. If your houseguest returns by then, she's welcome, as long as you're around to keep her under control."

"And unless you have shrimp, I'll leave the cat at home," Betty said, and hung up before Ted could query her about the cat.

Betty went out to the backyard. Tina followed her and then veered off to stalk through the grass while Betty headed to the back of the garage, where she could get a clearer view of the landscape. If Viola were roaming the fields and forests, she might be visible.

She stopped in the middle of her yard and gazed up into the still blue sky, thinking. Mandi had been murdered four days before. Tina hadn't had any shrimp for two days. Viola had left Tina at her apartment, she said, while she went off for a week. "I found her," Viola had said. "A horrible sight," she'd said.

Viola had been lying, Betty concluded. Viola Romanowski had told another *tiny* untruth. She *had* found the body. She'd been back to Manhattan earlier than she claimed. She'd bought shrimp for her cat. Betty scanned the fields behind her house, but there was no sight of Viola. Then she paused at the door of the garage. It had definitely been opened recently, to judge from the marks in the dry wood around the knob. Those Saks boys were devils all right. Neither their mother nor Betty would have been able to see them at their games out here. She went around to the front of the house and looked both ways on Timberhill Road, but there was no sign of Viola tottering along on her high heels.

What to do? When Betty started to feel uneasy, her usual procedure had been to resort to work and let the problem stir around for a while in the back of her mind. Often a solution or the obvious road became clear.

She went back to the manuscript, but she couldn't get out of her mind that Carole had warned her, inadvertently or not, that something was likely to happen. And Viola was simply impossible.

Tina meandered into the room, apparently feeling she needed company in order to lapse into a comfortable coma at Betty's feet. Betty stared at Crispin Abbott's precise handwriting, while the cursor on the screen blinked peacefully, waiting for Betty's input to move it along.

It was hard to concentrate on the words when so many other things were swirling through her head. Perhaps if she did something mindless, something to take her away from her thoughts. Well, she'd forgotten to bring in the morning's mail. It was something to do, and best to do that before the rain became too heavy. Halfway down the walk to the mailbox, dashing between the raindrops, she stopped dead.

Viola's car was gone. Could she have returned and driven it away without telling Betty? This was beginning to be very troubling indeed.

Betty had heard and seen nothing, but, of course, she'd been in the back of the house, in the dining room and kitchen.

The rain was coming down in earnest as she pulled her mail from the box and dashed back to the house.

She had to do something. She had to be sure Carole and Viola were all right. She was the competent one, the responsible person. She hated feeling uneasy and restless.

What she did was call the number of the Winfield farm, and again heard a rapid busy signal, as if the line were out of order.

She paced. She owed Crispin Abbott seven hours of work, a regular business day. She'd barely given him two hours. If she could manage another three today, she'd make it up the next day with nine hours. In the interim she would call Officer Bob about the women.

The front doorbell rang.

"I thought it better to come around instead of calling," Officer Bob said. He looked stern and imposing, and, of course, quite as good-looking as ever.

"Come in," Betty said. "I was working myself up to call you."

"About Viola Roman?"

"You know about her?" she said as she led him into the living room. "She was originally Viola Romanowski." The sight of the trooper spooked Tina, who had roused herself to groom her whiskers. The cat vanished behind the sofa.

"Nice to see you've got yourself a pet," Bob said. "Cats are good company."

"Not my cat," Betty said rather sharply. "Viola Roman's cat, temporarily abandoned on my doorstep. I don't like cats. I don't like dogs. I don't need a puppy, and I don't need a roommate. I don't need the problems of people I haven't seen in forty years or people I've known only a couple of weeks or for only five minutes. Sit down."

"Take it easy," Bob said good-naturedly.

"What about Viola?" Betty said. "Let's get that part over with."

"We had a call from the New York City police. Viola is involved in a murder in the city, she ran out on them, and they found your number at her apartment. They tried calling you, but you were out, so they called us. I take it she's been here. Why didn't you tell me?"

"Tell you what? She's a childhood friend who showed up last night at midnight with a tale of a murdered girl and people who were after her. She mentioned the police, but at that hour what was I to do? Viola always used to make up fantastic stories, so I took it with a grain of salt. Anyhow, the 'people' turned out to be media types whom she'd tipped off so they could turn the model's murder into a front-page story about herself. She used to be quite well known, and she thought she'd make some headlines once again. She was only going to stay the night, but then she confessed that someone was coming here to bring her something. That was early today. When I got back from town this morning, she was gone. She'd left her car parked on the road out there, and I just now noticed that's disappeared."

Then Betty took a deep breath, and said something she never thought she'd say. "I'm too old to have to deal with things like this. And Viola is too old to be behaving like someone in a second-rate thriller."

"Where might she have gone?"

Crispin Abbott was not going to appreciate it, but Betty said, "I'm doing some confidential typing for the man who now owns the Winfield farm, Crispin Abbott. I mentioned him to Viola, and she claimed she knew him in the days when she was the darling of the modeling world. I suppose it could be true. One imagines all well-known people know each other. I think she's gone there, although I don't know how she managed it. I tried to call him, but the line was busy. It sounded out of order." Betty put her hands to her head. "And now Carole. No one knows where she is either. After she called me about Johnny this morning, I went around to her house. She didn't go to work, but the neighbors saw her drive away. I know she was at the farm yesterday, because Abbott advertised for a model and she must have thought she was perfect for the job. Of course, Johnny Fender is staying there, so she probably couldn't resist going back to him. What a mess."

"So you think the two missing women are at the farm." Officer Bob probably didn't really care what Betty thought. "I've heard stories around town that it's really something now that it's been rebuilt."

Betty shrugged. "It's a pretty amazing place by anyone's standards. Not your typical East Moulton house, even compared to the big houses on Prospect Street. And it's very richly furnished. Crispin Abbott is, I suppose, a genuine character, but it's hard to imagine him welcoming both Viola and Carole with open arms."

"I'll take a run over to the place," Bob said. "See what I can find." He looked at Betty. "You okay?"

"Sure," she said. "This is just a bother. I have a lot of work to do. If you want a look at Viola's things, they're all over the place upstairs, mostly a vast collection of expensive cosmetics."

"Not necessary," Bob said. "At the moment the New York police just want to locate her so they can talk with her. They didn't indicate that they thought she murdered anyone herself. But . . ."

"Why does a 'but' spoken that way strike terror in the hearts of guilty and innocent alike?"

"The New York police provided a description of your Viola Roman. Are you sure she arrived here in East Moulton late last night?"

"Certainly. I still know what day it is, and I usually know what time it is."

"Nevertheless. Last night for sure?"

"For sure."

"I asked around town before coming out here. How do you suppose Molly Perkins recognized her description as a woman who asked for directions to Timberhill Road the day before yesterday? Molly assumed she was looking for the Winfield farm, not you."

"Viola was here before last night?" Betty was astonished. No wonder Viola had assured Betty that she could find the house. "Bob, I can't begin to analyze what Viola is up to. Or Carole, for that matter, but she's probably not as able to take care of herself as Viola, who has always seemed able to flutter her lashes through life and come out unscathed."

"I'll ask about Carole at the farm as well," Bob said. "Nobody's suggested she's done anything wrong, have they?"

"Of course not. I'm just concerned about her because of Johnny. Please tell me anything you turn up. There's also a girl named Sonia staying at the farm, although she was talking about going back to New York. Very pretty, tall, long straight blond hair. She seemed . . . troubled. I gather

Johnny had made a pass at her." She sighed. "I'm supposed to have dinner with Ted Kelso tonight, so if I'm not here . . ."

"I won't immediately think you've gone missing as well."

Before she returned to her computer, Betty had a thought. Rita. Someone would surely be around to answer the convent phone at this hour. Maybe Viola had decided to flee to her spiritual adviser. She couldn't have reached Boston yet, but she might have called ahead.

"Sister Rita Hayek please," Betty said when the phone in Boston was answered.

The soft Boston-accented voice said, "I'm sorry. Sister isn't here. She'll be back later."

"Would you ask her to call her cousin Betty? Collect." The sisters didn't like to waste precious funds on long-distance family chats. "It's sort of important." Then she added quickly, "Sister, do you know if anyone else called Rita today? A woman, an old friend."

"There was a call earlier," the sister said, "and Rita spoke to someone before she went out. Otherwise, I've been here all day, Betty. Oh, I shouldn't be so familiar, but Rita has mentioned you so often, we feel we know you. We're all praying that you'll come to visit us sometime soon."

"I'll try to come before long," Betty said. "Thank you, Sister."

"God bless you, Betty."

Betty replaced the receiver. She could never be the person Rita was, but she had a twinge of envy that Rita's idea of being needed was a focused kind of service. Betty's was scattered across the landscape now like those carefully raked leaves blown about by a random autumn wind.

CHAPTER 12

DANNY NEALON rubbed his forehead in a useless attempt to make his headache go away. Fred slumped in a chair across from him, looking as though he had a headache at least as bad. It was a gray New York day, but they might escape the rain.

They had just spent a difficult hour with a guy in a twelve-piece suit who admitted seeing Mandi Webb a number of times in the past three weeks, and who swore he hadn't killed her. He had come complete with a lawyer, scared but probably innocent of this particular crime. As he left, he'd said, "I admit to a taste for models, but Mandi wanted too much."

"Snotty yuppie stockbroker," Fred said when he'd gone. "I can't stand his type. Even if he didn't do it, he could have done it. A taste for models, he says. A taste! You'd think these poor kids were some kind of main course. The old filet mignon. These girls have no sense about the men they go out with."

"He was nervous," Danny said, "but there's no evidence he killed her. Nothing except that his name was in Mandi's Filofax. And he's married. Alison said Mandi had been seeing a married guy. In any case, he's probably scared somebody will find out he's cheating on his wife or his taxes, or doing some insider trading."

"Are they still doing that?" Fred asked. "I thought those boys had learned their lesson."

Danny looked at his notes. "The drummer in the rock band is no good. He's been on tour out west for the past two weeks, and she saw him only a couple of times. The rest of the names are professionals—photographers, hair and makeup men."

Fred leaned back in his chair and closed his eyes. "I still like the old girl. Viola ran. We know she was around the city when she said she wasn't, feeding her cat."

"Freddie, remember the window. Somebody opened it."

"The killer?" Fred shrugged. "Why would the killer come back?"

"Maybe to get something he left behind. And discovered that Viola knew . . ."

"So she ran because the guy is after her? She shoulda turned to us." He sounded very disappointed in Viola Roman. "Anything from the Connecticut police?"

Danny shook his head. "They promised to check out Betty Trenka. The trooper I spoke to said she's a solid citizen." Then he said thoughtfully, "The people at the agency have got to know more about Mandi than they're saying. People gossip. Henry Hamilton is more involved in the business than Rosellen let on. And if you ask me, Rosellen has to keep tabs on her models, if only to do damage control when something like this happens."

"Call it anything you like, Henry," Rosellen said into the phone. "You can call it a terrible tragedy. I call it damage control because somebody is going to find out that you were involved with Mandi and decide you killed her."

"I didn't," Henry Hamilton said to his wife. "I know Viola finally told you about me and Mandi. I'm sorry about it. What do you want me to do, Rosie?" Since he was on the other end of the phone, she couldn't see how tired he looked. He brushed back the wave of hair from his forehead. He had once briefly made a decent living as a model himself, but male modeling was not a milieu he had any taste for. However, his looks had held even as the years slipped by, and he was distinguished, weathered, and handsome. People said that he and Rosie were a gorgeous couple.

"Haven't you done enough?" Rosellen had put aside her business clothes and wore a casual Nicole Miller shirt, denim in front and lush silk printed with a witty design on the back. Her jeans carried a designer label. "I've done my obligatory statement to the press, and then I cut them off, but they're going to keep nosing around. I just hope the *Enquirer* doesn't think murdered Mandi Webb of the Rosellen Agency is a hot story. But I think I've figured out how to get you out of this."

"Me?" Henry spoke softly. "What about you?"

"I haven't done anything," Rosellen said. "Don't go pretending that I killed her. I've put up with your girls before. God, I have *such* a headache. And it's raining. You know what that does to my sinuses." Rosellen paused. "I knew that cunning little beast was going to cause me trouble."

"She was a nice kid. She didn't deserve to die, Rosie."

"Henry, don't start with me. I know what kind of kid she was, and so do you. I'll never forgive Viola Roman for bringing her around. One blessing is that once this is over, I will never have to speak to Viola again."

"It's not Viola's fault," Henry said. "She figured out about me and Mandi, but the price of her silence wasn't much to speak of. And look, Mandi wasn't a big name. People are going to forget this thing very quickly."

"Murder isn't easily forgotten, my dear." Rosellen's tone carried the barely suppressed rage Henry knew quite well. "Except perhaps by you. Just don't say a *word* to *anybody*. I'm handling everything."

"As usual," Henry Hamilton said. She couldn't see how troubled he looked.

He couldn't see how determined she looked.

The view from Crispin Abbott's studio with its vast glass wall was not what it could have been at midday. It was not what he had dreamed about when he first started renovating last spring. The sky was overcast, and the colors on the few remaining leaves on the trees on the facing hills were muted.

Crispin Abbott's mood was more than muted. It was black.

The day had brought him nothing but trouble. Sonia had vanished, probably gone back to New York without a good-bye. Johnny's girlfriend had showed up, and the two of them had gone off someplace. Abbott was afraid they'd gone off to fetch her things so she could take up residence in his house. He'd have to put a stop to that immediately. And she'd mentioned a child. Crispin Abbott shuddered at the thought of harboring a child. Bea had disappeared as well, so he couldn't even demand she make fresh coffee.

Then there was this one. He glared at Violetta reclining indolently on one of his fat leather armchairs with her feet on an equally fat hassock.

"Darling," she said, "are you sure you don't have a working telephone? I can't believe you don't have a cellular phone in a place like this. I could call the person who's to meet me, and wait here in perfect comfort. The minute I saw your fence, I knew I'd be safe."

Abbott did indeed have a cellular phone, and he didn't intend to allow Viola to stretch out her visit in waiting for some person she was supposed to meet. Instead, he said, "Are you sure I can't have Johnny drive you back to Miss Trenka's place, assuming I could find him?"

Viola refused to acknowledge his offer to return her to Betty. "Dear Betty. You couldn't have chosen a better, more loyal and conscientious person than Betty. That nice young woman who drove me here, Carole, thinks the world of Betty."

"I don't understand any of it, why she brought you here, why you came," Abbott muttered. "Look, Mrs.—Violetta . . ."

"I told you, she stopped to drop something off with Betty, and when I heard she was coming here, I thought a visit would be a lovely way to pass the time."

The buzzer from the gate rang faintly in the colonial room beyond the door.

"Don't answer it," Viola said. "It's the photographers,

and I can't face anyone just now. I shouldn't have allowed myself to hop into Carole's car without my makeup."

"I have no intention of answering," Crispin Abbott said. "I have no interest in those photographers." He scowled and paced before his window. "I do have work I ought to get to," he said, and ran his strong, stubby fingers nervously over his short-cropped hair. He stopped in front of a half-finished pastel drawing on an easel, Sonia semi-clothed and seductive.

"Don't let me stop you from working," Viola said brightly. "The creative process is so enthralling."

"And solitary," Abbott said, but Viola appeared not to understand. Sonia had probably hiked down to the main road and somehow found a ride to town. She couldn't have taken the Mercedes, since Bea had gone to town in it to shop. Johnny, especially brooding and ill-tempered this morning, had taken Carole away in the pickup.

If only someone would rid him of this Violetta woman who claimed to know him. She did seem to know certain surprising details of his life that he might have told her in confidence years earlier on some drunken evening at some wild party, the kind that used to make up a part of his life. But he doubted that he'd had an affair with her, which is what she seemed to imply without actually saying it. She also implied that she'd be willing to forget it for a price. Hah! He'd put a stop to that. Anyhow, thirty-five years was a long time. He couldn't remember everything. That's why he was writing his autobiography, but he was certain there was nothing about Violetta in his manuscript.

The bell from the gate rang again. He definitely wasn't going to risk an encounter with the press people he'd spied from an upstairs room, not while this ghastly woman who had brought them down upon him was still here.

"Darling," Viola said, "perhaps it's time for a noon aperitif. I wonder if there's a nice little wine—"

"No," he said firmly. "I stopped drinking years ago." He was not about to share his cellar of fine vintage Dom Pérignon with this woman.

"I am going to work out in the gym," he said finally. "Please touch nothing." Crispin Abbott was going to find his cellular phone, take it to a distant room, and call Betty Trenka, who was apparently the only sane woman in this town.

The resident state trooper sat in his car before the locked gates in the chain-link fence surrounding Winfield Farm. He'd tried the intercom, but there had been no response. Two large dogs padded quietly back and forth along the fence, keeping an eye on him, but they did not seem threatening. He had tried calling the number of the farm, but, as Betty had reported, it rang busy. The phone company indicated that there was a problem on the line; they'd look into it.

Officer Bob could see the top of the roof of the house beyond the trees, shiny from the light rain that had now virtually stopped. He thought he could see at least one car parked behind the protective trees, but there was no other sign that anyone was at home.

He started his engine, backed into the brush at the side of the old road, and turned around. As he drove back along the rough drive toward Timberhill Road, he stopped suddenly. Parked deep among the trees on an overgrown dirt track that had once been a road into the farm fields was a nondescript blue car. It was well-enough concealed that he hadn't noticed it on his way in. On the other side of the road was the old Winfield cemetery with its weather-worn white grave markers.

Bob was cautious as he got out of the police car, his hand close to his gun. . . .

"Hey!" A largish man rose up from among the tombstones and the tangle of wild roses, dead Queen Anne's lace, and poison ivy. "Oops," he said. "Officer, sir. Not trespassing, definitely not. Historical interest. Just doing my job."

Bob approached, noting the cameras, the large black umbrella leaning against an ancient tombstone that listed to the left. Now a young woman, also festooned with cameras, rose up from behind a gravestone.

"What exactly is your business?" Bob asked. "The owner is not welcoming to strangers."

"That's the truth," the young woman said sourly.

"We were looking for someone," the man said finally. "A news story, in a way." He fumbled in his garments. "I've got a press ID somewhere. . . ."

Bob nodded. "Don't bother," he said. "How long have you been here?"

The two looked at each other.

"Too long," the young woman said. "I'm damp and I'm freezing. It seems like hours."

"I mean," Bob said sternly, "*exactly* how long."

"We got here around ten. A lady down the road directed us. We went up to the gate, but nobody answered our call, nobody appeared. Nothing," the man said. "I wasn't about to go over the fence, not with those dogs."

"You didn't see anyone come or go? Nobody around the house?"

The two looked at each other again. "Not while we were here," the man said, and fidgeted. "Look, we left right after we first got here, because we thought we might have the wrong place, or maybe there was another way in. We weren't gone long."

"Wrong," the young woman said. "We were gone a long time. Anybody could have come and gone." She nodded her head in her colleague's direction. "Naturally, he got lost while we were driving around. We ended up back in the town by a circular route through the countryside. Then we had to stop for a burger. . . ." She sighed. "I'm ready to quit. Violetta isn't worth this pain." She sneezed. "Neither is Crispin Abbott."

"So you had no sight of Viola Roman, and you don't know definitely that she's here," said the trooper.

"Right." The man brightened. "You looking for her, too?"

"In a manner of speaking," Officer Bob said.

"The cops want *her*? She didn't say that—"

"What didn't she say?" the trooper asked quickly.

"She called our boss about that model's murder, and how she knew stuff about it. It was a couple days ago now. She said when she'd be here in this town, gave him the address where she'd be staying, but the lady at that house sent us here. Do the cops want her?"

"I'm just inquiring about her whereabouts," the trooper said cautiously. "Somebody was worried about her. The murder is not my concern." Officer Bob was tired of these two. "I have to go now." He wanted to find out from somebody what he was supposed to do next. Whatever had happened in New York, there was no crime in East Moulton, no missing persons report, nothing except these photographers and whatever Betty Trenka was saying about the missing women, whom he didn't consider missing at all. Did he suspect the worst? No. Besides, he had bigger problems in town to worry about, things the local constables weren't equipped to handle. The sudden rash of drugs at the high school was only one of them.

"You'd better go along now, too," Bob said. "If you're hungry, you should try a restaurant called Southern and Soul. Great ribs, sweet potato pie. It's on the way to the turnpike back to New York."

Whitey Saks, the oldest one, took the opportunity when no one was paying attention to sneak across School Street from the East Moulton grammar school and race down two blocks to the pizza place where the high school kids liked to hang out. The super-modern new high school that had just been built was farther along the street. In a couple of years Whitey would be in junior high and going to the big school.

Whitey's mind was on a bag of barbecue chips, firmly forbidden by his mother except under controlled dosage. He barely noticed the tiny girl clinging to the wrought iron railing attached to the three steps up to the pizza shop, but he stopped when she reached out and grabbed his leg.

"Whatyadoin'?" he said. She had to be a kid from the preschool attached to his grammar school, but Whitey knew enough to understand that although he *probably* shouldn't be there, she *definitely* shouldn't.

"Momma's coming," the little girl said.

"Yeah, good. You be careful. A lot of bad big boys and girls around here." Whitey knew that the kids who gathered out back in the pizza shop parking lot were up to big, bad high school things. He had a certain amount of daring, but that kind of danger didn't seriously tempt him yet. He was just a kid, but he knew enough to understand that he had to wait a couple of years before he could consider the bigger temptations of the parking lot.

"You should be over at the preschool with the rest of the kids," he said.

"The bus went," she said. "Momma's coming."

"You stay here and wait for your mother," he said. Since he was the oldest Saks boy, he'd had some experience giving orders to younger kids.

The little girl looked kind of scared, but she said, "Okay."

That was good enough for Whitey. He pushed his way through the crowd of high school boys two feet taller than he, and girls in big floppy shirts and black-lined eyes, and bought the forbidden chips.

The child was still outside when he left the place. Whitey gave her some chips.

"Hey, kid," somebody from the parking lot yelled. "You. Come here." Whitey gave him one quick look and then dashed to make his school bus home. If he missed the bus one more time, Mom threatened to lock up his bike for two weeks.

As the bus pulled out onto School Street with all three Whitey Saks boys on board, big Whitey saw the policeman's blue-and-white car cruise past and pull into the pizza shop's parking lot. The kids gathered there began to melt away. He hoped the policeman would see the little girl and make sure she got home. That thought made the vague nagging worry at the back of his mind go away.

By mid-afternoon Crispin Abbott finally admitted to himself that not only had someone disabled the phone system in his lovely house, he had also made off with his cellular unit. Johnny or Sonia—or even Bea Fender—had marooned him telephonically in this place with the impossible Violetta, who refused to shut up. A cruel, cruel joke to his mind.

There was a beat-up white car parked in his drive, which must belong to Carole, but the keys were not in the ignition, and he had never had the talent or training to hot-wire a car to get it started.

He did have the option of walking down the drive and then along Timberhill Road until he reached a friendly house where he could call Betty Trenka to rescue him, but the press monsters could easily be lurking still.

Anyhow, he had his image to consider, and besides, he didn't care for a walk in the rain.

When Johnny got back, Crispin Abbott was going to throw him and his dreadful mother out, along with the girlfriend and the alleged child. Violetta would go, too, even if she had to walk through the rain on her silly spike heels with her makeup streaking down her cheeks.

Crispin Abbott's mood was now very black indeed.

CHAPTER 13

AFTER HER unsuccessful phone call to Rita, Betty had pulled herself together and sat down again at her computer. Once she got started, the work flowed smoothly. The text, on the other hand, was beyond belief. Could Crispin Abbott actually have chatted with Albert Einstein about quantum physics? Did Picasso really teach him everything he knew about art and life and women? Was Chuck Yeager truly his best buddy? And how well could he have known Marilyn Monroe before and after fame encircled her? The first chapter alone was an indexer's dream: name after name after name. Abbott tended to ramble, but, Betty thought, this is *your* life, Crispin Abbott, if it's not all just a dream.

Nevertheless, work was good. It took her mind from the disappearances, which troubled only her. Officer Bob had not seemed disturbed by her information about the missing women, but who were they, after all? An out-of-town has-been model about whom the New York police had inquired. A young woman who was not highly regarded by her fellow townspeople.

Betty stopped typing. She ought to try to call Carole again. She did, and of course there was still no answer. She wished she'd gotten the telephone number of Carole's neighbor Sharon, to find out if Carole had returned to fetch little Noelle when the school bus brought her home. Or perhaps she'd taken Noelle away.

She answered the phone quickly when it rang, in the hope that it was Rita.

"Viola Roman?" She couldn't be sure if it was the same voice as the mysterious caller of yesterday.

"No," Betty said. "Who is calling?"

"Is she there?" The voice sounded distorted. It could have been male or female.

"Not at present," Betty said. She wondered if this could be the person who was to bring something to Viola.

"When do you expect her?"

"Who is calling?" Betty said again.

"An old friend," the voice said.

Betty thought quickly. "If you are the person Viola is expecting, I will give you a number to call where I will be around seven. I'll be able to tell you when Viola will be available." She gave Ted Kelso's number.

"You know about our arrangements, then?"

"Yes, yes, indeed," Betty said.

"I see." The person hung up, and Betty immediately dialed Ted and explained what she had done. "I have no idea where Viola is now, but I may know later. When the person calls, maybe we could tape the call on one of those recorder things you have and listen to it again. I apologize for involving you, but I couldn't think of anything else to do. I'm waiting for Rita to call—"

"Rita?" Ted managed to get a word in.

"My cousin the nun. I must have mentioned her. Viola might have decided to go to her in Boston without telling me." Betty pictured Viola's room upstairs. "Although I can't imagine her going anywhere without her makeup and her portfolio."

"I'll see you at seven," Ted said, "and I'll be evasive or, better, unavailable if a stranger calls between now and then."

"Good," Betty said with relief.

"You know," Ted said, "my life was quite even and serene before you moved in across the road. You seemed quite a sensible and retiring sort at first. I wonder now if your entire life has been lived in a state of high drama."

Betty laughed. "Hardly. Oh, I should mention that

Carole, the girl at the supermarket, seems to have disappeared. I do worry about her. . . ."

"Elizabeth," Ted said, "this is a quiet little town, and people are free to come and go as they please without reporting to you. I don't see any bodies lying around, do you?"

"No," Betty said slowly. She thought again about the little girl, and decided then and there to go back to Sharon's house to find out about Noelle and possibly Carole.

She wrote out a note to leave on the front door for Officer Bob and/or Viola, saying she'd be back by four o'clock. Tina circled her feet, rubbing against her legs as she got her trench coat from the foyer closet. The cat carrier had been crammed in to get it out of the way, and as soon as Tina spotted it, she ran for the hills.

"What's your problem?" she said to the cat, which was now peering out from behind the sofa. She was certain Tina scowled at her. "Food time already? Will that make you feel better?" She went out to the kitchen, opened another of the expensive cans of cat food, and dumped the contents into the saucer. To tell the truth, this stuff didn't look too bad. Tina seemed to find it just what the maître d' recommended.

Betty went out into the fitful rain, not enough to put up an umbrella, but the sky was heavy with clouds.

It didn't take her long to drive to Sharon's neighborhood, where all the dingy houses looked especially dreary under the dark sky.

"Wha—?" Sharon said when she answered the door. She may have been dozing. She was disoriented and weighed down by her pregnancy. "Noelle's not here. She must not have been on the bus, or she'da come here if Carole wasn't home. What time is it anyway?"

"Three," Betty said. "I was worried."

"Well, yeah. Sometimes Carole picks her up at preschool. No problem."

"Thanks," Betty said, and this time she got Sharon's number before she left.

School Street wasn't far out of Betty's way. It was tree-lined on one side, with old shingle houses and lawns, except for the intrusion of a pizza parlor and a variety store. On the corner was the brand-new cream-colored cement-block high school with playing fields spread out behind it. The old redbrick grammar school and the incongruously modern preschool annex were a bit farther along. As she passed the pizza place, she could see clusters of high school kids hanging out in the parking lot, off school property so they could smoke or do whatever was considered dangerously adult behavior for young people. Such gatherings were probably the source of Penny Saks's rumors about drug sales.

A nice, motherly lady in the preschool office was straightening out her desk in preparation for going home.

"Noelle? Why, she must have gone home on the bus. Let me think. I don't remember . . ."

"She didn't."

"Oh, dear. Then her mother must have picked her up. She sometimes does."

"I wonder," Betty said.

The woman stopped arranging papers in neat piles. "Your interest in Noelle?"

"I know her mother and have been trying to locate her all day." It occurred to her that Carole could have taken Noelle to Crispin Abbott's place. "I was concerned about the little girl."

"Ah. I thought you might be the grandmother. . . ."

"No," Betty said firmly. "Just a family friend."

"Everyone has pretty much gone," the woman said. "The buses for the little ones left a long time ago. I suppose," she added slowly, "you could call the police. They look for missing children, but that wouldn't reflect well on the school, would it? Especially since she's not really missing. I mean, the family hasn't said so."

"Her family is missing," Betty said patiently. "I don't mean to cause you problems." She gave the woman an encouraging smile.

"Why don't you leave your number. If little Noelle doesn't come to school tomorrow, or even if she does, I'll call you. How would that be?"

"That would be fine," Betty said, but it didn't feel fine even though someone else was at least half aware that all might not be well.

Outside, Betty looked back at the school building. Schools, she thought, fall into a kind of slumber when the students are gone. They had the same empty feeling that descended on offices when everyone had gone for the day. Betty had often worked late at Edwards & Son for just that reason: the peaceful, empty rooms with abandoned desks when the employees had been released to follow their private business, the glow of the overhead fluorescents in the halls outside dark offices.

She yielded dutifully at the stop sign where the driveway met School Street. The parking lot at the pizza place had mostly emptied and the blinking neon sign PIZZA GRINDERS SPAGHETTI blinked on and off as twilight approached.

Then she saw the child. She was standing on the curb in front of the pizza shop, turning her head slowly from side to side as though she feared to miss a familiar car coming to get her.

Betty eased out onto School Street and drove slowly until she was opposite the little girl. She rolled down the window.

"Noelle?"

The child looked at her. Betty had seen Noelle only that one time, but this was certainly she. There was a look about the child that recalled Carole.

"Momma's coming." The girl looked terrified, not so much, Betty thought, by the fact that she'd been addressed by name by a stranger as by the confusing, frightening spot she found herself in, alone on the street with no mother or friend in sight.

"It's okay," Betty said. "I saw you once with your momma. Remember? Would you like me to walk with you to the school? The lady is still there."

The child thought.

"It's okay," Betty said. "Your mother is Carole, some-times you stay with Sharon, and your house is yellow."

Noelle nodded. Betty got out of the car.

"Come along, Noelle," she said. Noelle took her hand tentatively and they crossed back toward the school build-ing.

No one was there. The door was locked, the lights were off. The motherly woman had departed.

"Well, Noelle. We'll have to go down the street and call Sharon. You like staying with Sharon, don't you?"

"She's getting a baby," Noelle said. "And she has a baby now. I want Annie." She looked a little tearful.

"Who's Annie?"

"My doll. Momma promised she'd bring her."

"She will, don't worry." Betty put Noelle into the front seat and puzzled how to fasten the seat belt for her. When she was reasonably sure it would hold, she drove to the first pay phone she saw, on the corner near the high school, and called Sharon's number.

Her hopes of finding a place to drop Noelle vanished when Sharon's brother-in-law said that Sharon was in labor, on the way to the hospital, and he was holding the fort and the existing baby until his wife got there. Betty looked back at the top of the blond head in her front seat, and wondered if she'd be charged with kidnapping if she took Noelle home to Timberhill Road.

"Would you ask your wife to call Betty Trenka? It's im-portant. Sharon's neighbor's little girl is staying the night with friends. My number . . ."

The brother-in-law didn't seem interested. She hoped he'd written down her number.

First a ghost from her past, then a cat, now a child. Could one of Frank Travis's golden retriever puppies be far behind?

"Do you like cartoons?" Betty asked when they got to her house. Noelle nodded, and Betty turned on the TV set. Tina strolled in and eyed the child sitting on the floor in front of the TV while Bugs Bunny cavorted on the screen. "And how about a glass of milk and—" She stopped. She wasn't at all suited to this. She reached out for the phone and dialed.

"Penny," she said, "I have a small problem here you might be able to help with."

Just before Betty was leaving to take Noelle across to Penny's house for the night, the collect call came from Rita in Boston.

"I haven't been so popular in years," Rita said. "First the New York police and then you. The police found my number at Viola Romanowski's apartment. There seems to have been some kind of mysterious death. They said it wasn't Viola. Is she all right?"

"That's why I called you," Betty said. "She was here, but she's not anymore. I thought she might have gone to Boston to be with you."

"I spoke to her a few days ago. She was upset about something, and started talking about sanctuary and the Church. I told her that was a difficult concept. Then she wanted to know if I had your address and phone. I couldn't imagine why, but I don't pry. I hope you don't mind if I shared them with her."

"No, of course not." Even though they'd known each other their entire lives, it wasn't easy to speak sharply to Rita. "How long ago was this?"

"I've been so busy lately. . . . When the weather gets colder, the shelter is overwhelmed. So many poor women who don't have a place to go. You and I are so fortunate in comparison. It must have been four days ago or so. What is going on, Betty?"

"I honestly don't know," Betty said. But she thought she knew why Viola had been upset. Three or four days ago she could have returned early to New York from visiting her friend and found the murdered girl.

"Viola never left off being the madcap girl of our youth," Sister Rita said. "Even now she isn't as . . . spiritual as she might be, although we do talk from time to time." Rita hesitated. "I'm not sure that what she's been doing is entirely"—Rita hesitated—"acceptable," she said finally. "She told me when she called that she wanted to make a substantial contribution to our shelter. She seemed to think she'd be getting a lot of money soon. Perhaps I shouldn't share our private conversation with you, but I didn't care for the sound of that. It sounded . . . well, it sounded very much like blackmail."

"Did she say anything about the death? The girl who was murdered at her apartment while she was away? It was four days ago by my reckoning, and although Viola claimed she'd been out of town, I think she knows more than she's telling."

Betty heard Rita breathe in sharply.

"No," Rita said at last, "she didn't mention murder. But she did say something like 'God is seeing that old scores are being settled.' "

"Old scores?"

Rita said gently, "I reminded her that God does not settle scores. We poor human beings forget that in our frailty we set up the conditions for old scores to exist. God is not a partisan, only our guide to the right path."

"And what did she say?" Betty saw that Noelle and Tina continued to sit peacefully in front of the TV set. She almost imagined that Tina was purring.

"Viola said that nevertheless, the score would be settled. I think her spiritual development leaves something to be desired."

"I had a nice Chardonnay to bring to dinner," Betty said when she arrived at Ted Kelso's front door at seven precisely, "but it vanished."

"Not a problem." Ted preceded her in his wheelchair into the dining area. Betty never failed to be impressed with the way Ted had arranged his living conditions to compensate for his disability. The open kitchen beyond the dining area was a marvel of convenience, with appliances, shelves, and bright copper pots and pans all at a level to enable Ted to reach anything from his wheelchair.

He led the way past the elegantly set table to the kitchen counter. "Pour yourself some of this truly terrific Burgundy," he said. "I take it your houseguest hasn't returned."

Betty sighed. "That's only the beginning of the tale," she said as she poured a glass of rich red wine. "Was it only last night that she arrived? Ah, this is delicious."

"Your Chardonnay wouldn't have been exactly right for the meal anyhow," Ted said. A handsome man with blue eyes and graying hair and that neat gray beard. "Tournedos with a bit of truffle, garlic mashed potatoes—a new recipe, by the way—and out-of-season baby asparagus from some very distant place where it is spring. Simple but expensive."

"Just the way I like it," Betty said.

"I have some nice pâté to start. So we'll start, and you'll tell me what comes after the beginning of the tale."

Betty repeated again in short sentences and reasonable order the bits and pieces she had shared in earlier phone calls and the matters she had neglected to mention. She told him about the telephone call from Sister Rita, and the hint of blackmail, and Viola's belief that some old score would be settled in the course of this adventure.

He listened as he grilled the tournedos and steamed the asparagus, sauteed the slivers of truffles for an instant in sweet butter, and tasted the garlic mashed potatoes.

"I wonder why the person seeking Viola hasn't called," Betty said. "I told whoever it was to try at seven."

"The person being blackmailed, don't you think? Man or woman?"

"I couldn't tell. Ted, aren't people being blackmailed dangerous to the blackmailer?"

"You don't have an answer to Viola's whereabouts anyhow," Ted said reasonably as he brought the food to the table.

"I wonder if that means the person knows where she is. Which is more than I do. She must be with Crispin Abbott, but why hasn't she tried to get in touch somehow? For that matter, why hasn't Crispin?" As Betty stared at her plate for a moment. "Why did Carole abandon her child? Of course, she might be assuming that Noelle is with Sharon."

"Wait," Ted said as he gestured to her to start her dinner, "back up to the child."

Betty said, "I forgot to mention the problem of the child." She explained about finding Noelle near the school. "I didn't know what to do with her, so she's staying the night with Penny Saks. Penny is thrilled to have a peaceful little girl under her roof to counteract the boys."

Ted thought for a moment while Betty savored her third bite of exquisitely tender beef. Finally he said, "I don't think one is allowed to scoop up a child from the street and take her home."

"I tried to leave word at the home of the woman who cares for her when Carole is working," Betty said. "But she's off giving birth and the man who answered wasn't too interested."

Ted pushed his wheelchair back from the table. "Be careful, Betty. There is a murderer out there vaguely connected with your friend Violetta. You've suggested to some doubtful people that you know about matters you actually don't know anything about. But since they don't know that, you could be perceived as a danger. As perhaps Viola is so perceived."

"She's blackmailing the murderer, then," Betty said slowly. "She must be. She saw what happened when she got home early."

He offered orange slices marinated in Grand Marnier and grenadine with a faint whiff of lemon zest for dessert.

"Viola must have made her way to Crispin Abbott's place," Betty said, "since she claimed to know him. The phone doesn't seem to be working, so I can't call. Officer Bob went to check, but I haven't heard anything from him either. At least the blackmail can't have anything to do with Abbott, and his house is fairly well protected."

"What was your impression of him? That was the original purpose of this dinner before other events overwhelmed us."

"Pretentious," Betty said. "An almost convincing liar when it comes to his life story. Ugly little man, but engaging, I must admit. Beautiful handwriting. He likes young, attractive female protégés about. He's lonely. Sonia, the girl who's there now, said he was merely paying for an entourage when what he wanted was a family." She sighed. "If Viola is there, at least she's got Sonia, and maybe even Carole."

As she pondered this, Ted left the table and wheeled himself rapidly toward the front windows which faced Timberhill Road.

"Ted, maybe I should drive to the Winfield farm and see what's happening. I know how to get past the locked gate. Yes, that's the only sensible thing . . ."

But Ted was not attending to her. He was on the phone, rapidly punching in a number. "Fire," he said into the receiver. "One Hundred Timberhill Road. You know? Good." He swung around and looked at Betty. "Don't worry. It's not your house. Only your garage is on fire."

CHAPTER 14

BETTY DASHED across Ted's polished wood floors to the window. At least Noelle was gone from the house. Only Tina remained.

Good grief, a roasted cat. How could she explain that to Viola?

"Calm down," Ted said. He had moved back to the window. "It really is only the garage, and here's the fire department already."

They could see the glow beyond Betty's house, and hear the sirens of the volunteer fire department trucks.

Betty took a deep breath and said, "I have to get Viola's cat. The garage is fairly distant from the house, but I can't leave . . ."

She grabbed her trench coat from the hook beside the front door. "Only yesterday I was wondering if the Saks boys had been playing in my old garage." She paused at the door. "I even wondered if they'd set it on fire someday."

As Betty crossed Timberhill Road, firefighters were descending from the two yellow trucks and heading toward the fire, lugging extinguishers. Three others were fastening a hose to the fire plug a distance up the road and uncoiling a heavy hose.

The neighbors were beginning to converge. Greg Saks with two of the three Whiteys, Molly Perkins and her husband just pulling up in their car, some vaguely familiar townspeople who had followed the fire trucks from town.

"Get back," a very young-looking fireman said.

"It's my house," Betty said. "And my garage."

An older man with "Chief" on his helmet said, "Nothing's going to happen to the house. We'll hose down the roof just in case, but I think it's confined to the garage."

"I can't leave my cat in the house," Betty said, and even at that stressful moment she realized that she'd said "my" cat.

"You can go in later if you want," the chief said. "But not just yet."

Betty looked around. Two youths on motorcycles had arrived to observe the fun. She thought she spotted Alida, her elderly neighbor, wearing a stately beige tea gown. There were several men and women she didn't recognize at all, notably a tall, striking woman who gazed at the scene thoughtfully, as though memorizing every detail. She seemed so out of place on this quiet country road that Betty was certain she was another media type summoned by Viola.

Then Betty spotted the jowly gray-haired woman she now knew was Beatrice Fender standing at the roadside almost smiling at the sight of the chaos surrounding the fire. Betty made a move to approach her; if she worked at the Winfield farm, she'd know if Viola and/or Carole were there. Bea, however, saw her coming and headed with unexpected quickness to a pickup parked a few yards down the road. Then Molly Perkins managed to push her way through the gawkers and corner Betty. "We were just closing up the pharmacy when the trucks went by, so I said to Perk, we got to see what's happening. Here's Bob. He'll tell us everything."

Officer Bob strode through the onlookers. He nodded to Molly, but took Betty aside. Molly's dismay was evident.

"The garage is gone," he said, "but your house is okay."

"That old garage was in bad shape," Betty said. "I was planning to clean it out, and now I don't have to. Not much harm done."

Officer Bob said, "Except for the body."

Betty stared at him. "What body?" she asked stupidly even as her mind turned over quite intelligently the couple of people nobody had seen for some time.

"We don't know yet," the trooper said. "The arson people will be here shortly."

"A body *and* arson?" She sighed. The Saks boys at play could have started a fire, but they had surely not matured to the point of leaving bodies about. "Could the fire have been started inadvertently, say by boys playing in the garage?"

Bob shook his head. "The chief has some arson training, and he and I both noted that the place had likely been doused with gasoline or some other inflammable. Unless your boys are serious pyromaniacs."

She shook her head. "Just boys. But what about the body? Even if someone were trapped in the place, all you'd have to do is lean on the door and it would fall off its hinges."

"It had been placed in an old trunk that didn't withstand the fire. In fact, the trunk was probably what was set on fire first. I'm not an expert, but I'd venture to guess that someone wanted to destroy the body of a person who was already dead."

"Oh, Lord," Betty said. "How awful." She took a deep breath. "Who was it?"

"I'd rather not say anything more," Bob said in an official voice. Then he relented a little. "It was a woman, Betty, but not much to recognize. They found a gold earring, I heard, and some bits of clothing, other indications that it was a woman."

"Ah." She felt a sort of sick apprehension. "Do they know if it could have been a tall woman?"

Bob shook his head. "No way of telling on the scene."

Which one? Betty shivered even as her mind raced. Carole was so young and hopeful, however misguided her hopes. And Viola, a link to her own past and, like Carole, full of misguided hopes. Then she was angry with herself. She should have taken better care of them. She should have kept a better watch on Viola, she should have guided Carole better. They had turned to her in need, and she had failed them.

Sid Edwards Senior's words came back to her: needing to be needed, that was her. Yes, Sid, she said to herself, I do need to be needed, and I should have done more.

"The fire's out," Bob said. The volunteers were making motions to pack up their equipment. "You can go into your house now."

"Bob, did you see Viola at the Winfield farm?"

"No one answered the buzzer on the gate. Some photographers looking for your friend had been there for a while and hadn't seen anyone come or go, but they could have missed something. Betty, I don't know exactly what's going on here, but I suggest you take care of yourself. The major-crimes men are going to want to talk to you. Don't try to hide from them the way—" He hesitated. "The way Viola Roman did."

"What an idea!" Betty said. "I don't know anything."

"I understand she told the New York police the same thing, and . . ." He didn't finish his sentence, but the conclusion hung there in the chilly night air between them: It could be Viola's body in Betty's garage. The woman hadn't gotten into the old trunk on her own. Someone had put the lifeless body there.

"Tell me," Betty said, "was it Viola?" He shrugged. "Then I will not be saddened now about a specific person. I will wait for confirmation." Another of her business tricks: Don't worry until there is something to worry about. But if it was Carole . . . "Bob," Betty said as he started to walk away, "I found Carole's little girl all alone after school at that pizza shop near the high school. I brought her home because Carole wasn't to be found. She's staying the night with Penny Saks."

The trooper frowned. "That would be a matter for the county child welfare people. I doubt if we could reach them now. Penny is as good a safe haven for the night as anybody. We'll have to deal with it, unless her mother shows up."

Betty and Bob looked at each other. It could be Carole, not Viola who never showed up again. Even as they looked at each other, the town ambulance crew, accompanied by two constables, were wheeling away the body bag with the person found in Betty's garage.

"I'm going back to Ted Kelso's house," Betty said, "after I check on the cat. We were having dinner, and he'll be wanting to know what's happened here."

"Be careful," Bob said again. "Remember the garage is off limits to everyone until we take a closer look by daylight."

"I understand," Betty said to Bob's back. He'd had a long day. It had been more than twelve hours ago that she'd spoken to him about Carole's early morning call about Johnny.

"Betty!"

She turned to face Penny Saks, one of the few remaining onlookers. Greg and the boys were gone, and Molly and Perk had departed, as had the striking tall woman she'd noticed. Only the boys with motorcycles remained talking to the firefighters who were coiling up hoses and stowing gear.

"This is terrible," Penny said. "Is there anything I can do? It must have been an awful shock. I know I didn't know what to think when Greg told me. . . ." She lowered her voice, although there was no one around to hear her. "Who was it?"

"They don't know who started the fire," Betty said, "although apparently it was intentional." And yes, it had been a shock. She was beginning to feel shaky.

"The body," Penny said urgently. "Everybody's talking about it. Was it little Noelle's mother? That's the first thing Greg and I thought. I mean, she has that reputation, and those people she hangs out with . . . You yourself said she was missing, since she didn't fetch Noelle."

"They don't know who it was," Betty said. "We'll have to wait. You didn't see anyone around my house before all this happened, did you?"

"I saw a few cars, but they had nothing to do with your

house. Of course, I didn't pay close attention. I was making dinner, and the boys were raising Cain as usual."

"I see," Betty said. Someone had come into her backyard from somewhere at some time with a dead body or a person who was to become a dead body. She suddenly remembered the light she'd seen at night while she was making up Viola's bed. Someone could have been prowling around her garage then. "I ought to check on my houseguest's cat, and then I'm going over to Ted's place for a few more minutes. Is Noelle okay?"

"Sound asleep. The boys just love her." Penny hesitated. "Big Whitey confessed that he saw her near the high school this afternoon, all by herself. She said her mother was coming, so he didn't think another thing about it. It must have been just before you found her."

"Penny, keep a close eye on her, will you? Maybe she shouldn't go to school tomorrow. Can you keep her at home for the day? Call the woman at the preschool in case Carole shows up." The two women looked at each other. "I had to tell Bob where Noelle was, so the child welfare people may become involved." Betty put her hand to her head. She actually did have a headache now; the aspirin she'd bought from Molly would come in handy. "Whatever am I saying? I can't ask you—"

"Don't worry," Penny said cheerfully. "I love having a little girl around for a change. We'll . . . we'll make a dress tomorrow. With lace and ribbons." She sounded like Martha Stewart discovering the best thing she'd ever dreamt up. "We'll stencil! Ducks!"

Noelle was in good hands.

Betty went into her house. The smell of smoke and dampness had seeped in, but it was nothing a good airing wouldn't get rid of.

Tina was not to be found in the living room or the kitchen.

"Kitty, kitty, kitty," Betty called, but that didn't work. She tapped a can of cat food against the kitchen counter. "Liver and turkey," she said. She listened and watched, but no cat appeared. She turned on the outside light over the back door and went out. A smoke-laden gust of wind hit her, but no lump of black-and-white cat cowered in the shadows. Her backyard had an unfamiliar look now that the garage was gone. The dark woods and fields stretched on without obstruction. She even imagined she could see the lights of the Winfield farm far in the distance.

"Come, Tina," she said rather sharply. Then she saw a human shape near the rubble of her garage and felt a twinge of real terror. Her heart beat faster. Even the worst moments of her long business life had never brought such a sensation, even when she had to face the man from the Internal Revenue Service with a stare like a Mafia hit man.

She stood exposed in the overhead porch light. The person was moving in the direction of the house. She ducked inside quickly and shut the door.

Whoever it was outside was polite enough to knock.

"Miz Trenka?" A young male voice. "Sorry if I scared you. It's Conrad Perkins. You know my mom and dad."

She peered out through the glass and saw a very young man in a semi-official-looking shirt. She opened the door to him.

"You did startle me," Betty said.

"I'm, like, an auxiliary constable," he said proudly. "The resident trooper wanted me to stand by for a couple of hours, keep an eye on the fire site. Murder site," he added, sounding pleased at the sound of the words. "They don't want curiosity seekers messing it up, even though they got it covered with a tarp."

"Wouldn't you rather keep watch from the house?" Betty said. "It's rather chilly out."

"No, ma'am," Conrad said. "I was told to stay right beside the garage, or what's left of it. Another guy's coming in a while to spell me."

"Could I make you some coffee? Only instant, but it would keep you warm."

"I wouldn't mind," Conrad said. He did look very young to Betty, but most people did nowadays.

"Did you know Johnny Fender?" Betty asked as she put water on to boil.

"Yeah, sure. Most of us kept away from him when we were in high school. They say he was dealing drugs when he left town for the last time."

"You mean after he'd come back with his new wife?"

Conrad looked at his feet and shuffled. "I don't think she's his wife, ma'am. She sure didn't act that way."

"And now he's back again," Betty said. "Have you seen him?"

Conrad shuffled again. "Guys are saying they've seen him up at Al's Good Times. The guys at the town police department are even saying he's mixed up with drugs again, over near the school. I haven't seen him myself. The girls were always crazy about him, no matter what he did." Conrad sounded as though Johnny's sex appeal, as compared with his own, was his most devastating crime.

"Here's your coffee," Betty said. "You can take the mug with you and leave it on the stoop when you're done. You haven't seen a black-and-white cat, have you?"

He shook his head.

"Well, I feel better knowing you're around," she said. Betty thought he looked so young and ineffectual that he might not be much protection, although he could probably handle an ancient garage that had burned to the ground.

"I'm only seeing to the scene," he said.

"Nevertheless," Betty said, "I'm sure you are most capable." One of her Edwards & Son rules: Praise, give responsibility, and get results. It could work here. And since the young man's mother was Molly Perkins, it could be difficult for him if something went wrong on his watch. "I'm going across the street to Mr. Kelso's for a few minutes, after I find my cat."

Conrad returned to his post, and Betty went upstairs to search for Tina.

She pushed the half-open door to the guest room and switched on the lamp.

"Ah!" she said aloud. The room was in perfect order. No

traces of Viola remained, no clothes strewn about, no un-made bed. No suitcase, no portfolio, no makeup case. In the bathroom the makeup and flagons and brushes and bottles were gone.

She nearly stumbled in her haste to get down the stairs. Viola had been erased from her house, and the cat had been kidnapped. She sank onto her sofa. She needed to collect herself before she went back to Ted's and get over the idea that a stranger had been in her house.

Then she almost laughed in her great relief. Viola herself must have been there, taking away her things and her cat for reasons unknown, and had not felt it necessary to in-form Betty.

Suddenly Betty was alert. She heard a faint but unmis-takable meow, and then Tina emerged from behind the sofa and marched to the middle of the room. She glared at Betty as though all of this were her fault.

Betty leaned down and looked the cat straight in its stern yellow eyes. "You may not believe this, but I am quite pleased to see you." And then she wasn't. If Tina were still there, it meant that it couldn't have been Viola who re-moved everything. Viola would not leave her cat behind.

She tugged open the foyer closet door which had a stick-ing problem from the day she moved in. She found the cat carrier where she'd shoved it into the back to get it out of the way.

If someone had tried to erase evidence of Viola, the at-tempt had failed. Betty still had the cat. If the body that had just been taken away to a cold autopsy lab was Viola, that someone might well decide to come back for Tina to re-move the last bit of evidence that Viola had ever been in East Moulton. Even if Viola were alive, the same might hold true.

The phone rang, and Ted said, "I think you ought to come back. There are matters we need to discuss."

"Quite a few things," Betty said. "I just need to . . . I'll be right over, and I'm bringing company. Viola's cat. Someone cleared out all of Viola's things except the cat, and I don't want to leave it here. It can stay in its carrier and won't be damaged by the experience except for raising its normal crossness level."

"A cat won't trouble me," Ted said.

"Well, it troubles me," Betty said.

She pulled out the cat carrier and opened the top. Tina hissed. It was not going to be easy to deposit Tina in the box, since that was clearly associated with the disliked rides in the car. Betty looked inside the carrier and saw that it wasn't empty. She lifted out a plastic shopping bag from the East Moulton supermarket. Inside she found a worn rag doll, pink pajamas, some little girl's underwear, jeans, T-shirts, and a new-looking dress. There were also a half dozen sandwich-size brown paper bags, and in each was a plastic bag full of—

Oh, no, she thought. She'd seen enough movies, read enough newspaper reports, viewed enough news stories on drug busts and drug deals to conjecture immediately that the white powder she was looking at was some illegal substance. What was Carole up to? These were surely Noelle's clothes and her longed-for doll, Annie, but drugs were more than she could take in. Penny Saks had talked about drugs at the high school. But Carole? Then she wondered when these things had been left there.

It must have been when Betty was out during the day, or while she was at dinner with Ted and people were setting her garage on fire.

If it were that morning while Betty was in town depositing Abbott's check, Viola was still there. Viola wanted to see Abbott, and here was a person with a car who knew where Abbott lived. Violetta could certainly coerce a young woman in awe of the glamorous life to give her a lift. While Viola was upstairs putting on her makeup, Carole was downstairs looking for a place to stow the clothes and drugs. She'd get them from Betty when she picked up Noelle at school and she wouldn't have to return to her house in case someone she didn't want to see was waiting for her.

She thought again. Where would Carole get drugs in this kind of quantity? Johnny Fender was the likely candidate, and also likely to be involved with bodies and arson.

What a mess, Betty thought. She put the plastic bag high on the closet shelf, then thought again. She'd have to tell the authorities about the drugs, if that's what they were, but she wasn't going to leave them where she found them. After a moment's thought she stowed them under the sink in the kitchen, in among the cleansers and the drain opener and dishwashing liquid. Then she faced the business of transporting Tina.

There was a small tussle involving the carrier, but Betty emerged unscathed except for a tiny scratch on the back of her hand.

CHAPTER 15

THE SMELL of the fire still hung on the air, suspended in the damp night, but it was fainter now, almost a memory.

Ted's front door was off the latch when she walked in with the cat carrier, eager for his calm reasoning to help her sort out the question of the body, the elimination of Viola's presence, the child's clothes, the cat that had been left behind.

Ted was not alone.

"Elizabeth," he said from the far side of the open room, "there's someone here you'll be interested in seeing."

"Viola?"

A tall woman rose from one of Ted's classic and comfortable Stickley chairs.

"Not exactly," Ted said.

Betty immediately recognized the woman she'd seen watching the fire. She walked toward Betty with exceptional grace, her short curly hair reddish in the room's subdued lighting. Casually dressed in pressed jeans and a deep purple silk warmup jacket, the woman put out her hand to Betty.

"Miss Trenka, I've been terribly upset about Violetta."

Betty did not sense any terribly deep emotion behind her cool exterior. She took the woman's hand briefly, noting the large gold ring with a silver crest on the middle finger. She blinked, but the woman had drawn her hand away.

"This is Rosellen," Ted said from his place at the far side of the room. "Rosellen Hamilton. Is that the cat?"

"What?" Betty was distracted by Rosellen's cool, superior smile. "Yes. The cat."

"Set it free," Ted said. "If my chair runs over its tail once, it won't let it happen twice."

"I'm an old and dear friend of Violetta's," Rosellen said. "From New York."

Betty bent down to unlatch the cat carrier. Tina emerged scowling and hissed in Rosellen's direction before speedily finding refuge under the desk holding Ted's computer terminal.

"I had the most peculiar telephone call from my husband," Rosellen said, "saying that I should rush here to help Viola out of some difficulty. Fortunately, I was here in Connecticut at our weekend home in Litchfield."

"A lovely area," Betty said to give herself a moment to collect her thoughts.

"We wanted to be sure she was all right."

"Why would you or your husband think that she wasn't?" Betty asked. "Something to do with that murder in New York?"

"Ah," Rosellen said smoothly, "of course you'd know about that."

"Of course." Betty took off her trench coat but kept it over her arm. "And you know where she was staying."

"She told us. She said you two were great friends. She has a gift for friendship, don't you think? We've, too, been close to Viola for years."

Quite an eloquent fabricator, Betty thought, and wondered if she should confront Rosellen with her little lies. By her reckoning, Viola had discovered Betty's whereabouts from Rita only a few days before, and had made a reconnaissance trip to East Moulton while she was supposed to be in New Jersey. Piecing together Viola's tales seemed to indicate that she was too busy discovering a body and fleeing the police to chat with Rosellen Hamilton, unless . . . An idea was forming that had to do with that other body.

"And now . . ." Rosellen's voice had a catch in it, and

she appeared, to Betty's wondering eyes, to be wiping away tears. "Now she's gone."

"Gone?"

"The fire. You heard that they'd found her body."

"I heard nothing of that," Betty said. "A body was found. I prefer to think it was not Viola." She looked at Ted. "Mrs. Hamilton must have shared the news."

Ted nodded.

"But I was certain I heard . . ." Rosellen frowned and returned to her chair.

"There are a number of possibilities," Betty said. "And hundreds more nobody had thought of. Other than you," she added pointedly, "literally no one knew that Viola was in East Moulton. Wishful thinking has perhaps led you to hear things." Rosellen blinked, and Betty said, "I should say, rather, your imagination has caused you to think you heard—Viola," she said firmly, "is off visiting a man called Crispin Abbott, who has recently taken up residence just a mile down the road."

Ted said, "You must know him. Everybody does."

"I don't," Rosellen said. "Unless you mean that awful man who's always in the papers."

"The very one," Ted said. "Very rich. Very celebrated."

"I think we may have met," Rosellen said. "Imagine him being here in this very town. Of course Viola would be drawn to him. She thrives on the mere idea of money." She stood again. "I do thank you for your kindness. I'm so glad I saw your lights and you gave me sanctuary." Ted was gazing at her with a bemused expression as she gestured with her long, graceful hands, taking in the pleasant, tasteful room.

Ted said, "It's getting late, Mrs. Hamilton, and I need my rest." He tapped the arm of his wheelchair feebly, as though he had reached the limit of his strength. Betty looked away to hide a smile. Ted was the least self-pitying person she knew, but he was devilishly clever about using his disability to rid himself of unwanted people.

"I'm *so* sorry," Rosellen said. "I must be going. I'll be

back in Litchfield in an hour." She turned to Betty with an unreadable expression. "I'm so relieved that Viola is all right."

"As are we all," Betty said.

"Elizabeth," Ted said, "since you'll be going as well, you'd better find the cat. It seems to be hiding over there."

"It's not very friendly," Betty said. "Cats can be nervous around strangers. You'd know that, Mrs. Hamilton."

"I don't really care for cats." She bent down and picked up a large leather and canvas carryall from the floor behind her chair. Betty watched her move gracefully toward the door, head high. "I'll let myself out," she said, and put the straps of the carryall over her shoulder. "My car's just outside. Good night."

Betty watched the door close on Rosellen Hamilton. "Ted, would you believe that that woman was in my house tonight while we were having dinner here?"

"I could believe that," Ted said. "I could believe a recent encounter with an unfriendly clawed creature, a cat, say. She has a scratch on her hand."

"I told you someone had removed every one of Viola's possessions, and the scratch, taken with what looked like Viola's big black modeling portfolio in the bag thing of hers, leads me to believe that Rosellen erased Viola from my house, but Tina wasn't about to be erased. Rosellen hadn't been able to find the carrier in the back of the closet. She could have learned where Viola would be if Viola had a reason for telling her. She could be the person Viola was expecting . . ."

"Your mysterious caller?" Ted nodded.

Betty nodded. "Twice. Rita said that 'it sounded like blackmail,' when Viola spoke with her, and who would Viola be blackmailing if not the murderer?"

Ted put his chin in his hand and thought. "Blackmail is dangerous, and I judge Rosellen Hamilton to be about as dangerous as they come if someone crosses her. She has the will to do anything, if I can still judge character," Ted said.

"Then she could also have had the will to murder poor

Viola tonight, and put her body in my garage and set it on fire. Viola might have come back while I was here for dinner, and found Rosellen waiting. Once she's dead, Rosellen gets rid of all signs of her."

"Except for the cat," Ted said. "And, of course, you're still here to say Viola was at your place. Crispin Abbott, if that's where's she's been, is presumably still here to say the same."

"I ought to go to the farm," Betty said. "I won't be able to rest well unless I know whether both Viola and Carole are there and both are alive. Ah, Ted, here's an odd thing, or a frightening thing, however you look at it. I found a bag of Carole's little girl's clothes hidden in my closet. She must have left it while I was out, and might have been planning to pick them up there so she wouldn't have to go back to her own house. And, oh, yes, there appeared to be quite a large amount of some white powder that could be drugs. Johnny was said to be involved with selling drugs around the high school."

"In that case, do not think of going to the farm," Ted said vehemently, quite unlike his usual tone. "You can't risk it."

"What risk?"

"Are you pretending to be obtuse? If Johnny Fender is about, if he or your friend Carole stashes drugs in your house, if people connected with the farm are turning up dead. . . . And if that's not sufficient, if anything you suspect about Rosellen is true, she's probably not on her way to Litchfield, she's probably lurking around the neighborhood, or actually proceeding to Crispin Abbott's place in search of Viola—if she didn't kill her and now believes that nobody else did either. That's why you shouldn't risk it, you stubborn woman."

"I think that last part is far-fetched," Betty said.

"Then consider this. Rosellen hints that her husband also has some interest in this. He allegedly sent her off to look for Viola, so he, too, could be lurking somewhere nearby.

That is why you can't risk going. Too many theoretical adversaries."

Betty thought for a moment. She remembered Molly's remark about the man who asked directions to Elizabeth Trenka's place today. Perhaps Mr. Hamilton had entered the picture after all. Then she had a moment of enlightenment. "You may be right. The blackmailed person is not necessarily the one who committed the deed for which the blackmailer wants money. I see. I don't know Mr. Hamilton, but on paper, and sexist though it sounds, a man would be far more likely to be involved in a situation with a beautiful young model. A situation, I mean, that involved ... heightened emotions, leading to murder. Viola would know something about Mandi's relationships. Now Rosellen is prepared to help her husband by buying Viola's silence."

"As you say," Ted said, "it looks good on paper. So please don't pay Crispin Abbott a visit tonight. There are too many potentially dangerous unanswered questions in the air. We'll take our suspicions to the police in the morning. Now, sit."

Betty sat at his command with her trench coat still over her arm and her sensible shoes dampened by the rain and the runoff from the firemen's hoses. Dampness always made her hair frizz and escape from the neat bun at the back of her head. Ted wheeled himself around sharply and started removing the last of the dishes from the dinner table.

"Can I help?" Betty asked.

"Just sit still and organize your thoughts. Consider all your reasons why going to the farm are bad ones."

"You're right. Poor Viola," Betty said. "We went back a long time. I'll have to call Rita."

"Elizabeth," Ted said firmly. "You don't know it was Viola, so don't get emotional. It doesn't suit you."

"There have been occasions," she said almost defiantly. "I am human."

"Then be reasonable. Call the state trooper in the morning and tell him what you think. Have him pick up the alleged drugs. Call the farm and ask for Violetta. And if you don't like the idea of being alone at your house tonight, you could stay here. The guest room is made up, not that I encourage many guests to stay."

"I couldn't," she said. "I'll be all right. Besides, if someone's out to erase me—Rosellen, for example—she'd just come here, and I couldn't involve you. I'll be all right. The police have posted a sentry of sorts to watch over the garage." Not that she thought Conrad Perkins was a match for a murderer.

"That's something," Ted said. "Just be careful. Do you have my number programmed to speed-dial? The police?"

"I never bothered. I can still remember phone numbers."

"I don't doubt it," Ted said. "But do it when you get home, just in case."

Betty lugged Tina back across the street one more time. There were no mysterious cars parked on the road, no shadowy figures lurking in the bushes near her front door. She was too exhausted to check whether Conrad or his replacement was still guarding the ruins of her garage, but she went out to the kitchen to be sure the door was firmly locked.

Then she did try calling the Winfield farm. The phone rang this time, but no one answered.

Tina circled Betty's legs, apparently none the worse for her frequent traveling.

"No food," Betty said. "You've had enough." To tell the truth, she had no idea how much a cat the size of Tina needed to eat. Tina's desires, however, were plain enough. "You've seen a lot of bad things lately, haven't you?" One murder, at least, and one break-in, and goodness knows how many people attempting to carry her off.

Tina seemed resigned to having no late-night snack, and ran a paw over and around her ear. Betty's headache, which had retreated at the sight of Rosellen Hamilton, returned as a nagging throb in her forehead. If she acted now, at almost eleven o'clock, would she be able to save someone else from an awful fate, or had the worst already happened? The police knew where Viola probably was, or had been, and they didn't seem intent on acting on it. They also didn't seem especially concerned about Carole, although they knew that her daughter had been abandoned, in a manner of speaking.

Well, they had a body, they would find out who it was, and then they'd go into action. Dead was dead. There was nothing to be done right now with regard to the deceased.

No knowing, however, was worrying.

Then Betty thought she'd better go to bed. Tina was remarkably docile, although remarkably weighty, as Betty lifted her and carried her up to the bedroom.

"Better stick together," she said. Tina blinked, leapt from the floor where Betty had placed her, and found a spot on the corner of the bed to settle on.

Betty didn't even try to think about what she'd do tomorrow. Then she remembered that she was committed to volunteering at the library the next day. It was all too much. She closed her eyes and willed herself into a deep sleep.

CHAPTER 16

THE LAST beer drinkers left the East Moulton Bar and Grill, having talked over and over the fire up on Timberhill Road, and the dead body they'd found. A couple of the men were volunteer firemen who'd stopped in after the fire, so there were plenty of tales to take home.

Someone wondered about that woman who'd bought the house on Timberhill Road, the place Molly Perkins's uncle used to own.

"I hear she paid a good price," one man said. "These foreigners, never know what they'll do."

"Come on, Frank. She's from up around Hartford. It's not like she just got off the boat from somewhere. If you want a real character, take a look at the guy who bought Winfield farm. He did pay a fortune."

"He keeps women there," someone else said. "Bea Fender says the goings-on are something terrible."

"Give us a break. Bea Fender drove her old man to drink and then he hit the road just to get away from her. I don't set much store by anything she says. And that kid of hers is a bad one. I'm surprised nobody shot Johnny years ago."

"Somebody got shot?"

"That's what they're saying. Up at the house on Timberhill Road, the old place near the Winfield farm."

"You know, I heard from Bea that the farm is stuffed with gold."

"And I heard—remember the construction workers who worked on the Winfield place?—I heard they practically

148

tore the house apart and rebuilt it so's you'd never recognize the old dump."

The pack of men edged through the door of the bar and grill one by one.

"My granddad used to say those old Winfields buried their gold with them in the old cemetery on the property."

"And my granddad knew the last of the Winfields, and not one of them had a dollar to their name. Nothing but the old farm. It's the new fellow there who had the dough. Johnny told me himself. He's in tight with the new man."

The men stood outside on the chilly, damp street as the proprietor turned off the lights behind them.

"That boy's back in town? Johnny's bad news, that one. Remember that drug business got him run off five, six months ago? And that girl of his. A tramp, my wife says . . ."

"I don't know what to make of all these new people in town. Anybody know anything at all about them?"

"No good can come from having foreigners," Frank said. "I better be getting on home, fellows, 'fore I catch hell from the little woman. . . ."

The good townsfolk of East Moulton scattered and walked off into the night. The town shut down early, and except for some comments to drowsy wives about the fire put out, the body found, and all these people nobody really knew, it was all put to rest for the night.

In a nice little house on a tree-lined street in the borough of Queens, New York City, not really all that far in miles from the apartment where Mandi Webb had died in her pretty pink nightgown but very far in spirit, Danny Nealon lay in the dark beside his sleeping wife and tried to forget for a few hours that the case of the murdered model was getting out of control.

The tabloids had jumped on the story with all the accompanying headlines. It didn't help that Violetta was fairly well remembered, so it was a delicate matter to keep from admitting that the New York police didn't exactly know where she was.

The police also didn't exactly know where the head of the dead model's agency was either. Rosellen Hamilton had left town for her weekend house in Connecticut, her office had said, and she had become virtually unreachable for the moment. She was supposed to be interviewed again by Danny and Fred. Her husband, Henry Hamilton, was also floating around somewhere. He wasn't at their Manhattan apartment, but no one could say where he was.

The Connecticut State Police hadn't been able to locate Viola Roman, but the East Moulton trooper had spoken to the woman she was supposed to be visiting. Apparently this Betty had suggested that Viola was visiting one Crispin Abbott who'd settled nearby, but no one was presently at home at his house.

Crispin Abbott was someone people knew. One of those guys who were famous in their own mind and famous in New York. Over the years he was said to have extracted a lot of money from the unsuspecting newly rich who thought his artworks were worth something. Now he was living up there in that little Connecticut town to which Viola had fled, but nobody could figure a connection between him and Mandi Webb.

All these people know each other, Fred had said. Maybe.

Danny felt himself drifting into sleep as he pictured once more the two Violas—the stunning woman in the photographs on the wall and the aging beauty he'd seen in person. Sad in a way. "Skin-deep doesn't last," his mom used to tell his sisters, "and you'll be crying for years over what you've lost if that's all you have."

How true.

Danny would pull it all together tomorrow.

Fortunately for his night's sleep, Danny didn't know yet about the body in Betty Trenka's late garage.

The old Winfield farm still attracted old ghosts to marvel at the expensive renovations that had left only some ancient wide-planked wooden floors, darkened beams, a few hints of former rooms: The shades of bearded and bent men who'd torn rocks from the fields in order to sow their crops; work-worn women who'd hauled water from the pump for their washes and for scrubbing those wooden floors; boys and girls bundled to their eyes who trudged down the hill past the family cemetery and along the country road to their schoolhouse . . .

Such things as were to be seen today at the old place were galaxies away from the old life of the farm.

The Rhodesian ridgebacks scratched at the door with the lion's head knocker, but their plea to enter the warm house went unheeded. In the heart of the house, a TV picture soundlessly showed endless opportunities to buy gold chains, Capodamonte candle holders, a sparkling pantsuit in larger women's sizes for glamorous winter parties. . . .

Crispin Abbott dozed in an easy chair beside the swimming pool cunningly hidden away in a room in the heart of the house, where the TV played and the mirror behind a mahogany bar straight out of a classic ocean liner reflected potted palms and cut-glass decanters and all manner of dark-green-and-gold luxury from another age, brought together by clever and attractive interior designers. The border of the pool was carpeted in green, and the rest of the room in Oriental rugs. The wall lighting sconces dripped with crystal pendants.

The pump in the pool thrummed quietly as the green water in the pool circulated through the filter.

Abbott jerked awake and shook his head to clear it.

How the hell did I come to this? Crispin Abbott thought. That damned Violetta woman is to blame, I know it. She started in on Johnny and that girlfriend of his with all her airs, and then she'd had the temerity to argue with them.

The next thing he knew, those two kids had forced him and Violetta down here and had locked them in. He hadn't known that Johnny had a gun.

What had become of Violetta, anyhow?

She'd demanded that the girl allow her the use of the bathroom outside the pool room, and that had been what seemed like hours before.

Then Johnny had said Sonia was gone for good. Lovely Sonia. Maybe the impossible Violetta was gone, too, leaving him there.

He could only hope that Johnny and Carole and that monstrous Beatrice would simply rob him and depart, with him locked in the pool room in the old cellar of the Winfield farm instead of dead as well. Surely Betty Trenka would try to reach him sooner or later, and he'd be released.

"I hate this business," said the young woman in the dirty blue car parked on the drive up to the Winfield farm. "Nobody's going to be roaming around here at night. Nobody's going to get a picture of this Violetta out in the rain. Give me a break. I don't care how many bodies they find."

Her companion felt on the floor near the driver's seat for the bag of sour-cream-and-onion chips he'd stowed to help him through the night.

"She could be the one they found dead," he said. "And since she was supposed to be up here at this Abbott's place today, he could be the murderer. Think of what good shots of him would do for us."

"Okay," the young woman said. "You stay awake for the next couple of hours, and then it's your turn to sleep. Yuck, this place smells like a Burger King nightmare." She rolled down the car window to let in some air. "And that cemetery is scary."

"Forget it," the man said. "No ghosts are coming out in the rain. You think anybody's really at home up there? Not a light in the place since it got dark."

"Somebody better be there," the young woman said, "or I quit tomorrow. That woman in the station wagon swore Viola was still there, since she wasn't dead, whatever that means. We could have told her she wasn't going to get through the gate."

"What do you say," the man said, "I leave you up by the gate for a coupla minutes while I run into town for coffee or something. Just in case somebody shows."

The young woman's response was not agreeable.

* * *

"No," Betty murmured in her sleep. "No more . . ." She could barely manage to open her eyes, but once again the insistent ringing of the telephone was dragging her into wakefulness. She fumbled in the dark to find the bedside phone.

"Hello?"

A woman's voice said without greeting, "Mrs. Roman is staying the night with friends."

"Who is this?" Betty managed to say.

"She is leaving in the morning and she will call you."

"Where is she?" Betty said.

"Mrs. Roman is staying the night with friends. She is leaving in the morning and she will call you."

There was a click and, after a moment, a dial tone.

Betty struggled upright and turned on the bedside light. She could almost have sworn it was a message that had been recorded. She looked at the phone in her hand. She couldn't have dreamt it. Tina raised her head, and her yellow eyes caught the light. Betty hung up the phone and fell back on her pillow. She lay still for a moment, catching the last faint whiff of damp smoke.

What sort of game was this? Was it a genuine message from Viola? In that case, she was alive. She was not the body in the garage.

Betty reached over and turned out the light. Viola must be playing some silly game, and was probably staying at Crispin Abbott's house. There were certainly enough bedrooms to house her in luxury. And if she'd retrieved her belongings except for her cat, she'd have her makeup to put on in the morning.

Where would she be leaving for?

Then Betty remembered the portfolio in Rosellen's bag. She'd assumed that it had been Viola's, but perhaps all aging ex-models carried pictures of their glory days around with them.

Still, she ought to mention it to Officer Bob. . . .

Betty sat up suddenly in bed, causing Tina to bound heavily to the floor in alarm.

Suddenly, she was almost certain who the body in her garage was.

A gold earring, Officer Bob had said.

Well, some kind of ring anyhow. How about a trendy little fashion statement worn by a pretty young woman in a turquoise bikini? A little gold naval ring. Sonia had been wearing such a ring.

Her first sense was one of relief. It hadn't been Viola or Carole out there in the trunk after all. Viola actually was staying the night somewhere. Carole was all right, even if she'd been terribly irresponsible in her treatment of her little girl.

Then, in the midst of relief, came sadness. What, Betty wondered, had poor Sonia done to deserve death?

Sitting there in the dark, as Betty considered her belief that it was Sonia who was dead, she felt equal certainty that it could only have been Johnny who put her in the trunk and set the place on fire. And she could have been put there as long ago as the night Viola arrived, when she'd seen the light in the garage.

And what, she wondered, as she lay back again, will they have to say about all this at the Winfield farm?

The combination of the strange mechanical-sounding message about Viola and her sudden realization about Sonia were not conducive to a quick return to sleep. She lay in the dark, staring up at where the ceiling was, although it was too dark to see it.

Johnny had grown up in East Moulton. He had surely known the house that Betty had ended up buying had been empty for a time. He'd left town before she arrived, and learned that the house was now occupied only on his return. Perhaps somewhere in the mess that previous tenants had abandoned he had left something of value to be retrieved on his return to the town.

Once retrieved, her foyer closet was a handy temporary hiding place.

And somewhere in that mess of a garage was a place to hide a body and then try to destroy it completely.

Suddenly, Betty held her breath. She was certain she had heard a noise from downstairs. She knew she'd locked the back door, but she couldn't remember if she locked the front and thrown the deadbolt. Forgetful again, and when it really mattered.

There was definitely a sound from below. Her bedroom door was slightly ajar to allow Tina to leave if she chose to. Betty raised herself on her elbows. Tina was obviously not a watch cat. She was curled up at the foot of the bed, untroubled by any untoward sounds.

Then she heard a noise she recognized: the sticky foyer closet door resisting being opened.

All right, she thought. Enough is enough. She was weaponless, but she had surprise on her side—plus a guardian just outside the back door. Conrad wasn't likely to be armed, but he was an ally, if he had managed to remain awake.

She got out of bed quietly and didn't bother to seek out her robe, but glided as quietly as possible in her sensible blue flannel nightgown. She edged out the door. From the doorway she could see a small wavering light from below, some sort of flashlight. She moved forward to the top of the stairs and peered around the corner down the stairs. Someone must be looking for the packets of drugs or whatever that had been hidden in the closet. She wouldn't risk a direct confrontation, but, nevertheless, the situation had gone too far. As soon as the person left, she'd call the police.

All at once she froze. Unmistakably, the odor of gasoline drifted up from below.

Now she was angry. She was not about to have her house set on fire by some desperate character who went around wreaking havoc in this peaceful old town. She balled her hand into a fist and began beating on the wall with all her strength when shouting as loudly as possible, "Out, get out! Get out now! Out!"

The surprise worked to a degree. The flashlight was dropped from the look of things, retrieved, and turned out. The intruder was no longer making an effort to keep quiet. Betty advanced to the head of the stairs, still shouting and banging on the wall.

Tina, perhaps in some vain hope that the commotion signaled a midnight snack, tore past her in a headlong flight down the stairs, making her contribution to the din.

Suddenly, the front door opened and Betty briefly caught sight of a figure in dark clothing fleeing into the night. Betty stumbled down the last few steps and hurried to the front window. She could make out the shape of a car speeding away with no lights.

Betty turned on the lights in the living room. The foyer closet door was open, and the floor in front of it was strewn with Noelle's clothes. The cat carrier was in the middle of the floor, its top open.

Foiled, Betty thought grimly.

The smell of gasoline was strong but not overpowering. She found the uncapped metal canister near the closet, but the intruder had not gotten to the point of spreading the gasoline around the room. She replaced the canister's cap with the edge of her nightgown, wondering if what she'd heard vaguely about preserving fingerprints was true.

What to do?

She refused to believe that Carole would set her house on fire with her in it, but she had no such doubts about Johnny Fender, based on his reputation. At the same time, what did she know of Crispin Abbott really? Or Rosellen Hamilton, for that matter.

Or even Viola.

There was no sign of her so-called guardian out by the garage. Let him sleep.

She turned all the lights on on the ground floor, turned on the television, and carefully locked the front door. She brought a blanket from the bedroom and curled up on the sofa. Tina seemed mildly put out that she'd been rudely awakened and that there were no instant treats to soothe her temper. Betty was unwilling to indulge her.

She managed to sleep a bit on the sofa as the television showed *Headline News*, repeating the newsworthy events of the preceding day a good four times before the sky began to lighten a little in the east behind the clouds that hung heavy over Timberhill Road.

CHAPTER 17

As MORNING arrived, a cloud seemed to come right down to the earth outside Betty's house. It wasn't exactly a fog and it wasn't quite rain, but in any case, morning had come without the sight of the dawn.

Tina sat in front of Betty, who was still on the sofa, and stared at her expectantly. She looked remarkably like a cat designed by Fernando Botero.

"Something has got to be done," Betty said, "but I don't know what."

Tina marched toward the kitchen, no nonsense about her now.

Sonia dead in the trunk in her garage. Viola missing, with her false eyelashes and preposterously high heels. Carole drawn back helplessly to Johnny, completely forgetting her child.

Rosellen with the mark of Tina on her hand drifting about the state of Connecticut, if not the immediate neighborhood.

Someone had planned to burn down her house with her in it.

And finally, Crispin Abbott was silent. That was quite troubling in itself. He had been so insistently eager for praise of his autobiography. Yet when she was unable to call him as she'd promised because of the out-of-order telephone, he had done nothing to reach her. Surely he had a means of leaving the farm even if his phone was inoperative. She understood that everyone in the world except her had cellular phones nowadays. He could even have gone out to find a working phone or have taken the trouble to discover where she lived and gone there.

Something was badly wrong at the farm.

The woman who answered the phone when she called the resident trooper's number was someone on duty from the town police department. She knew nothing about the dead woman, and said so in a tone that asked, Even if I did, who are you that I should tell?

"I need to speak to Officer Bob," Betty said, and gave her name and number. "It's urgent."

"Oh, right. It was out at your place that it happened." But she sounded suspicious, as though Betty herself could be a murderer. "People are supposed to be out there today to look at the crime scene, and there should be somebody on duty now."

Conrad Perkins or one of his ilk was not what Betty had in mind.

"Thanks," Betty said. "I'll check on that."

She briefly contemplated trying to reach someone with the New York City police to tell what she'd intuited about Rosellen, her husband, and the murdered model, along with Viola's probable blackmail plan. However, she hadn't been in business as long as she had without knowing that if you failed to convey information to the right person, that information was likely to be hopelessly lost in translation. She might do her duty and ease her conscience, but to very little avail.

With Tina fed and now reclining on the area rug near the heating vent in the floor, Betty went up to put on jeans and a sweater and pin her hair extra firmly to keep it under control in the dampness. She put on her sturdiest leather Bass Weejuns and stuffed the pockets of her loden coat with money, keys, and her driver's license. She cast about for some sort of defensive weapon, but all she could think of was the small Swiss Army knife she usually carried for minor emergencies.

She was going to the Winfield farm to check out the lay of the land.

Downstairs she peered out the kitchen window. The guardian of the ruins was not anywhere in sight in the mist. Even Conrad would know enough to come in out of the rain, or at least manage to stand under the eaves to keep dry. She opened the back door, and sure enough, a miserable-looking young man—not Conrad—was huddled close to the house. Conrad's empty coffee mug was on the stoop.

"I understand the investigators are coming," Betty said. "I have to go out for a while, but I'll bring you some coffee first."

The youth nodded. He was clearly praying to be relieved of his post, and clutched the hot mug Betty handed him.

This is foolhardy, she thought as she started the engine of her car, but no one else seems to be doing anything about the situation at the farm.

In any case, she was just going to have look, nothing more.

She drove slowly along Timberhill Road, past Alida's grand house surrounded by black-limbed, leafless trees. There was no traffic on the road and no sight of human beings. It was still too early for the children to congregate for the school bus.

As she neared the mailbox that marked the road to the farm, the pickup truck that was associated with the place careened out of the side road onto Timberhill Road, swerving just in time to avoid hitting Betty's car. Bea Fender was at the wheel with a kerchief around her head. The vehicle sped away toward town. Betty was mildly shaken by the near miss as she slowed to make the turn to the farm. At least someone was up and about at the Abbott place, if only Bea.

Suddenly, the dirty blue car that belonged to the press photographers bounded and shuddered out from the side road and tore off in pursuit of the pickup. The plumpish man and the young woman in the front seat did not seem to notice Betty, so intent were they on following Bea.

The media hadn't given up, but Beatrice Fender alas

wasn't going to make a sensational front-page story in the *National Enquiring Star* or a dramatic video segment on a nighttime TV tabloid show.

Betty caught her breath, settled herself, and turned onto the road to the Winfield farm.

The dark, leafless trees lining the rough road dripped heavy raindrops and seemed to lean in over Betty as she drove carefully toward the house. The old cemetery—her first sight of it by semi-daylight—looked ghostly in the mist.

She braked suddenly at the sight of something moving among the weather-worn headstones. All at once from the underbrush galloped the two dogs from the house. They gamboled playfully around Betty's car, evidently delighted at their cleverness at having escaped beyond the fence around the house. Bea must have been in a great hurry to leave the gate open when she raced away in the truck.

In the rearview mirror Betty saw that the dogs were following her up the hill. She shook her head. What a muddle, yet the sight of Bea rushing off on her business was somewhat of a relief. Apparently, life was going on at the farm.

On the other hand, some of that life had ceased. She couldn't forget that it was certainly Sonia who had died and been placed in the trunk.

The gate in the chain-link fence was wide open. In the drive in front of the house she saw a battered white car, but there was no sign of the Mercedes.

When she got out of her car, the dogs romped around her eagerly. Indeed, their enthusiasm for her seemed excessive, since she was someone they'd encountered only once before. The rather large animals circled her, tongues lolling and eyes fixed on her.

She paused. Her experience with domesticated animals was extremely limited. Indeed, Tina was about it. But she got the message. The dogs were hungry, human beings provided food, and Betty was the most convenient human being in sight.

Hungry dogs meant that no one had fed them today or

even longer. Bea certainly had not fed them before she left in a hurry, but where were the others—Johnny or Crispin?

The house before her was silent. She hadn't seen the place by day, but now she could see that only parts of it even referred to its early days: rough timber and stone here and there, but it had been greatly expanded with modern additions in order to fit the interior she'd seen briefly. In any case, a great deal of money and labor had been invested in lonely old Crispin Abbott's country retreat.

She went toward the front door cautiously, although the frolicking dogs did not aid her attempt at a stealthy approach.

"Now, stop it," she said firmly. "Sit."

Miraculously, they sat. They fixed their eyes on her and did not move.

"Good dogs," she said softly, and for good measure said again, "Sit. Stay."

They sat, they stayed.

Betty raised her hand to lift the lion's head knocker, then stopped. Instead, she turned the doorknob carefully. The door swung open. She heard the dogs make a move behind her to enter, so she quickly stepped inside and shut the door behind her. Under the circumstances, it couldn't hurt to let them suffer a few more hunger pangs until she'd discovered what was up.

In the half-light, the colonial room appeared as it had on her first visit, except that a pile of cartons was stacked up in the middle of the room: boxes that had once held dozens of cans of tomatoes from Italy, bunches of bananas from Costa Rica, quarts of dishwashing liquid from Cincinnati. Grocery store boxes, in short, taped up haphazardly or tied with heavy twine.

It was almost as if Crispin Abbott had decided on the spur of the moment to pack up his treasures and abandon the farm. Somehow she doubted that.

Betty heard the dogs whimpering and scratching at the door, but she hardened her heart. When she spotted a telephone on a quaint spindly-legged table, she lifted the receiver. Dial tone. At least she could now reach the outside world if necessary.

She listened. There was no sound anywhere in the house. Even the dogs seemed to have given up.

Betty picked up a heavy iron poker from a rack beside the fireplace. It was better than nothing. Then she went through the door into Crispin Abbott's studio, only to gasp and take a step backward as soon as she entered the room and saw the faint, ghostly figure in the distance.

Then she relaxed. It was only her own reflection in the expanse of glass that formed the wall of the studio, illuminated by the light in the colonial sitting room behind her.

It seemed unwise to turn on lights in the studio, since that would leave her exposed to the great outdoors and anyone who might be out there in the pale, misty morning.

Instead, she prowled carefully around the room in the half-light.

There were no bodies, alive or dead, in the fat black-and-red-leather armchairs. She stopped briefly at the unfinished drawing of poor Sonia. No one except Betty yet mourned her. No one except Betty mourned the lost souls who seemed to be involved in some intricate, puzzling pattern of deceit and death: lonely Crispin Abbott and, most of all, Viola, or, rather, the old Violetta, who'd succumbed to the march of years but was still frantically trying to be what she once was.

Since there was nothing to be found in the studio, Betty started back toward the door, then stopped and squinted through the dimness. The shelves along the wall that had been crammed with Abbott's colorful collection of objects and fabrics were mostly empty. She edged around for a closer look. The floor below the shelves was littered with broken bits of turquoise, red, and blue glass, as though someone had in haste knocked unwanted vases, bowls, and goblets to the ground as the shelves were cleared.

This was an ill omen surely. Crispin Abbott would not have destroyed his treasures so carelessly.

Betty, still clutching her fire poker, slipped away from

the room and into the colonial fantasy. The house was still deathly silent. She tried to remember the route of her brief tour of the house. Through that doorway, she knew, was a hallway that would bring her to the long dining room with its monkish refectory table and then on to the huge kitchen. Short steps up from the end of the hall led to the wing of sitting rooms, luxurious bedrooms, and marbled baths. She wanted to be careful that she wasn't trapped in some cul-de-sac. There must be people somewhere, even though Beatrice Fender had departed.

Then, for the first time, she paused to wonder where Bea had been heading at such speed. Racing away from some terrible situation in the house, or merely on an urgent errand to buy bread and eggs and pastries for breakfast?

The dining room seemed especially gloomy, but it, too, was empty. The kitchen with all its stainless-steel cabinetry and butcher-block counters was also empty, but here there were signs of human existence. Remains of meals on dirty plates, a few used glasses, some empty beer cans, were scattered about on the counters. Careless housekeeping on Bea's part, or else something far more important had turned her mind from her appointed tasks.

As Betty made her way toward the stairs to the bedrooms, she noticed that there were empty places on the wall where paintings had hung. A glass-fronted case was stripped bare. She'd remembered seeing on its shelves the collection of intricate gold artifacts and jewelry that Crispin Abbott had called the essence of the artistic skills of the Inca and the Mochica. She had even reminded herself at the time to look up the history of the ancient people who'd made such wonderful objects. Everything was gone, probably packed up in cartons near the front door.

The iron fire poker gave her small comfort as she looked into the bedrooms. The masculine bedroom with a huge African sculpture in one corner, which Crispin Abbott had mentioned was his room, was empty and orderly, with the bed made, blinds up, and the curtains open. No one had recently slept there, unless the bed had been made up at an impossibly early hour. In two of the other rooms the beds were disorderly, as though people had slept on the coverlets. The other bedrooms were untouched. The sitting rooms were neat.

In one of the spacious bathrooms, where she dared to turn on the light because it was windowless, she saw the first sign of Viola. Her bright blue coat was hanging on a wooden hanger over the shower curtain rod.

So Viola was here, or she had been.

On her way back to her starting point at the front door, Betty glanced out the window at the top of the stairway and saw the dogs racing around the lawn. Apparently, they had decided to forget their hunger and play on Crispin Abbott's carefully created lawn. Although it was still overcast, the mist was beginning to dissipate, and she could see the view over the fields to distant hills lined with ranks of trees whose remaining leaves had been swept away by the rain, interspersed with clumps of fat evergreens.

Time was passing. The only places left to look were the gym and the pool room down in the basement of the old farmhouse.

CHAPTER 18

In New York City, Danny Nealon learned of the unrecognizable female body found at the house of Elizabeth Trenka in East Moulton. Although it as yet had no identity, it was certain that it was the body of a young woman of average height.

"Not our Violetta, then," Danny said to Fred Carver. "She's still on the loose."

Fred looked disgusted. He was in a terrible mood, and every time he looked at his older daughter he imagined her getting into the same kind of trouble as Mandi Webb and ending up dead. He was almost convinced that moving someplace far away from New York City was a good idea.

"We don't know that," Danny said. "Even more interesting, Rosellen Hamilton is not at her house in Connecticut, where she said she'd be. Well, Freddie, with everybody keeping an eye out for Viola, she's going to be found eventually. She's too distinctive to blend into the crowd. We'll figure out Mandi's murder soon enough."

But not for a while. More immediate demands—one of them the apparent suicide of an Upper East Side society wife—claimed their attention right then.

"Viola may have missed her moment in the headlines," Danny said as he and Fred set off. "This other one's a big story. Poor Viola."

"She'd get it back," Fred said philosophically, "if she'd confess to murdering Mandi."

* * *

Penny Saks got the three Whiteys ready for school while Noelle sat quietly at the kitchen table on a pile of phone books, eating her oatmeal. Noelle was reduced to wearing some jeans and a T-shirt the youngest Whitey had outgrown, and Penny was quite anticipating the prospect of buying her a few bits of little-girl clothing to tide her over until her mother turned up.

Penny was incensed at the idea of a young mother leaving her child that way. If these girls don't know how to raise a child properly, what was this world coming to?

She caught sight of the several plain dark-blue-and-black cars that had converged on Betty's house. The police investigators for sure, and one of them had even brought a pickup, probably to cart away the evidence. In spite of the awfulness of last night's discovery of a body and the fire, Penny was quite thrilled by the goings-on. She'd wait a while before she called Betty to find out what had been discovered.

"Have you had enough, honey?" Penny asked Noelle.

Noelle nodded, hesitated and said, "Is Momma coming?"

"Pretty soon," Penny said as casually as she could, and rather untruthfully. "She has some important business to take care of. Do you know what that means?"

Noelle nodded again, this time uncertainly.

"We're going to have lots of fun today," Penny said. "First we'll go out to the mall and buy you a nice new outfit."

"I don't have Annie," Noelle said.

"Annie?"

"She's my doll. I always have Annie when I sleep."

"Then we'll find a nice doll to take Annie's place for a few days. Okay?"

"Okay," Noelle said, and got down from her chair. She went over to a window that looked across the field to Betty's house.

"Johnny," she said. "Is Momma there?"

Penny said a mental "uh-oh." She wasn't going to surrender little Noelle to Johnny Fender. Why, she didn't even refer to him as her daddy, which seemed to confirm that the child wasn't his.

She looked out the window over the top of Noelle's blond head, but all she saw were a couple of middle-aged men in business suits and a state trooper in uniform who wasn't Bob, and the cars and the truck that had parked there earlier.

"Johnny's not there, honey," she said. "Your momma's coming later."

Sharon had given birth in the early morning hours to a seven-pound-eight-ounce girl. Her sister-in-law, at Sharon's home caring for the other baby, had no time to worry about her husband's scribbled note about a neighbor's child who was being cared for by some woman in town. She didn't think much of Carole anyhow from what Sharon had told her, and she knew all about Johnny Fender. He had a reputation all over this part of the state.

The investigators from the state police went to work in the ruins of Betty's garage. There wasn't a great deal to do or much to see. They took away a few bits of what remained in the garage, but they decided not to trouble the lady of the house so early. The local resident trooper was going to come around with one of the major-crime men later in the day.

Rosellen Hamilton looked across the cramped room at her husband, who was standing at the heavily curtained window of a significantly inexpensive motel off the turnpike a few miles from East Moulton. He was peering out through a crack in the curtain at the gray morning, that youthful wave of hair falling across his forehead.

Rosellen paced in front of the undistinguished bureau marked with old cigarette burns, now and then glancing at herself in the distorting mirror behind it. "I *know* she's there, Henry. I can sense these things, but I wasn't going to risk being recognized by those press people." She almost stamped her foot in annoyance. "I had the money and I was ready to pay her off."

"Then kill her off, I suppose."

"Henry . . ."

"Only in a manner of speaking, my dear."

"How dare you say that when you don't hesitate to kill. That little slut Mandi has ruined everything—us, the business, everything."

"You're wrong, Rosie. You continue to believe that I killed Mandi Webb in a fit of passion, and I say I didn't." He turned around and looked at her. "I continue to believe that you killed her."

"Well, I didn't, not that she didn't deserve what she got. The important thing is Viola believes that one of us did it, and she says she has proof she can take to the police. Even if it's no proof at all, the woman won't keep quiet, I know it, unless she has the money. If the police don't believe her, some press idiot will. She's got them stirred up already."

"Then we should go back to Crispin Abbott's place. An unpleasant little man—at least the couple of times I met him."

"Crispin's all right," Rosellen said. "He wasn't to my taste."

"Another old romance that didn't work out . . ."

"Stop it. You have more than your share of old romances. And no, we're not going back to that house. We should stick to that unattractive woman friend of Viola's. That's where she'll come back to."

"You took away all her things."

"I thought we'd find her, and could send her on her way. But the cat is still there. That's where she'll go."

Henry Hamilton watched his wife gaze thoughtfully at the ceiling.

"If she doesn't take the money and run," Rosellen said, "we may have to take other steps. I'm not going to let her get away with settling old scores so easily."

CHAPTER 19

As BETTY crept through Crispin Abbott's self-indulgent house, she reminded herself that life in East Moulton was going on as usual, and that soon enough she'd be rejoining it. It was foolish of her to be there; she should be sitting at her computer, typing out Crispin's words and drinking her second cup of good coffee.

But there was still Viola and Carole to consider. People didn't get lost that way if everything was all right.

She opened the door to the gym. All the black-and-chrome equipment before her was a complete mystery. She knew about dedicated working-out only from the pictures of muscular biceps and triceps and thighs glistening with sweat on television commercials.

There was no one in the room, but on the windowsill were what appeared to be empty whiskey and vodka bottles. Perhaps this was where Bea Fender came for her nips.

Finally there was the pool room, down a flight of narrow steps. She moved especially carefully because, if she recalled correctly, this definitely was a cul-de-sac. The way in was the only way out.

The door to the pool room was closed, as was the door to its left that led to a shower room and lavatory. She turned the knob on the pool room door, an old-fashioned glass doorknob faintly lavender colored. She remembered ones like it in the old family house in Cattonville. They were high-priced antiques nowadays. The door didn't open, but then she saw the big metal key in the keyhole. It turned with a ponderous click and she cautiously opened the door a crack.

She looked in through the narrow space, breathing a waft of chlorine-scented air. One light was on in the room, and the water in the pool on the raised platform had a ghostly green glow. The dark furniture and green carpeting gave the place the look of an ocean liner, just as she remembered from her tour.

Betty heard no sound, so she opened the door wide and stepped into the room.

Suddenly, she found herself propelled backward by the force of Crispin Abbott attempting to overpower her and bring her down. She lost hold of the poker, and her glasses flew off, but she managed to keep her balance.

"Stop!" she gasped. "Wait . . . Betty!"

Abbott ceased his attack. The startled expression on his face was almost worth the alarm she'd felt under attack.

"Betty," he said stupidly. "Where are the others?"

"I am indeed Betty," she said as she retrieved her glasses unbroken from under an end table. "There aren't any others here that I could find."

Crispin scrubbed his cropped head furiously in a nervous gesture. The pool pump continued to hum, the palm fronds swayed a bit in the circulating air. "They were going to leave me here? For eternity?" he said in disbelief.

"Oh, I don't think—"

"It's what *I* think that matters," Abbott said. "No one's here? Not even that god-awful woman you sent here?"

"Viola? This is where I thought she went, but I tell you, no one's in the house. Only the dogs are outside, and they're pretty hungry."

"No Johnny? That girl of his must be around. And his mother."

"I saw Beatrice Fender driving away in the pickup," Betty said. "Have they done something to Viola?"

"I can only hope," Abbott said grimly. "And what about me? Definite psychological damage. I doubt that I'll recover." He took the key from the door and pocketed it.

"They locked me up in here last night with that Viola woman. Moans and groans and saying she was being punished for her sins. She had to reach a sanctuary. I don't know what Johnny and the others were up to."

"Among other things, packing up all your valuables," Betty said. "And possibly invading my home in a search for drugs."

Abbott cocked his head. "You into drugs?"

"No, no," Betty said impatiently. "Johnny or Carole hid some away in my house to be retrieved later. Shall we go now? They may come back. We ought to try to find poor Viola."

"Poor Viola nothing. That Carole was outside guarding the door while the boyfriend was busy robbing me. I kept hoping that Sonia would show up to save the day."

"Sonia's dead, Crispin. I'm sorry. I'll explain later. What about Viola. We can't hang around here too long."

Crispin looked stricken by the news of Sonia, but went on bravely. "Viola raised hell about needing to use the facilities," he said delicately. "It's right outside, so the girl led her away, and that's the last I saw of either of them. A mixed blessing," he added under his breath.

"Let's take a look," Betty said. She picked up the poker and headed out of the pool room, a bit apprehensive about what they would find in the shower room.

What they found was Carole sitting on the floor, her hands tied behind her back to the pipes of an old-fashioned porcelain sink. Her mouth was taped with shiny beige packing tape that was also wrapped around her head and her frizzed hair. There were tearstains on her cheeks, but her eyes were furious.

What Betty found most interesting was the fact that Carole's hands had been tied with Viola's long dark blue scarf.

"We ought to take the tape off," Betty said.

Carole winced as Abbott removed the sticky tape from her mouth.

"That old bitch, I could kill her" were her first words.

"And don't dare try to take the tape off my hair. It'll ruin it."

"Viola is very resourceful," Betty said.

"But not kind," Abbott said. "She did leave me in the pool room when she could easily have freed me."

"Untie me," Carole demanded. "I've got to go to Noelle. Sharon won't keep her forever."

"Noelle is staying with my neighbor. Sharon's off having her baby," Betty said. "You'll have to stay here a little longer. Where's Johnny? And his mother?"

"I don't know," Carole said. "Bea went off somewhere last night. Johnny went out late last night, too, to . . . to find something."

"Drugs hidden at my house by you," Betty said. "He didn't find them, and he didn't have a chance to burn my home down the way he did my garage. Or kill me the way he killed Sonia."

"What? Johnny killed Sonia?" Abbott was shocked.

"He didn't kill Sonia," Carole said sullenly. "It was an overdose or something. She pestered him for drugs, so he gave them to her to shut her up. Then he didn't want to leave the body here."

"My little Sonia? Back to drugs? I thought that she'd be okay here, away from that world, but it followed her here. And therefore Johnny did kill her, young lady."

"Please let me go. I didn't do anything," Carole said. She slumped back against the sink.

"We'll lock her in the pool room," Abbott said, "while we see about ourselves. Promise to go quietly?"

"If you promise to get me out of this," Carole said sullenly. "A big deal, Johnny said. Easy money. We'd take the Mercedes, pick up Noelle, and hit the road with all the gold and stuff from this house."

Between them, Betty and Abbott took an unresisting Carole to the pool room.

"There's soda in the refrigerator, some crackers left that I didn't eat," Abbott said. "Sit."

Carole sat in one of the armchairs beside the pool as they locked the door behind them.

The house was still apparently empty.

"What could have become of Viola?" Betty said. "She seems to have a taste for disappearing, and every time she does, I imagine she's dead."

"It would take a stake through the heart to finish off that woman," Abbott said. "Talk, talk, talk. Famous this and fabulous that, and she was a match for anybody when it came to coming out ahead. Lots of money coming her way, if she could get back to your house, she told Johnny that to his face. That's probably what he was looking for last night as well as drugs. And then there was her makeup, she couldn't survive without her makeup case, she looked a wreck. . . . And her precious cat. Ah!" He caught sight of his stripped case that had contained the gold artifacts. "That evil boy."

"The cat, the makeup," Betty said thoughtfully. "And Rosellen's money. Crispin, I suggest you call the police. I'm going."

"Going? Going where?"

"To find Viola."

"And where do you suppose Viola is?" Abbott accepted the fire poker from Betty although he appeared not to know what to do with it.

"I'm not certain," Betty said, "but I believe she's driving a pickup truck. Don't forget to feed the dogs."

CHAPTER 20

VIOLETTA, AKA Viola Romanowski, aka Viola Roman, aka . . . all those other names she'd carried for shorter or longer periods over the years, was furious. She looked *frightful*, and someone had taken away all her makeup. The case was gone, her clothes were gone, and all she had were a few little bottles and brushes in her handbag. Someone was going to pay for this.

It was, to her mind, worse than murder.

At least darling Tina had been in capable if unappreciative hands.

Her photographers, bless them, hadn't given up, but where on earth was Rosellen? She'd promised she'd be in East Moulton with the money last night. Of course that dreadful episode with those vicious children had caused a delay, but fair was fair. Rosie had better turn up today, or she'd be facing some trouble.

Rosellen had had enough experience with the perfidy of men to believe anything of Henry, up to and including murder. Viola had known for ages that Henry had been seeing Mandi, who was certainly irritating enough for anyone to murder.

Mandi hated Tina and she'd stolen little things from Viola, and, worst of all, she'd dismissed Viola's entire career as an old-fashioned lark. That was when Viola had had the big photo of herself on the Spanish Steps framed and put smack in the middle of the living room.

The very worst thing of all was that Mandi was going to go to Rosellen and tell her about her affair with Henry.

That would have stopped the nice little income flow from Henry which was the price of Viola's silence.

The thing was, Henry must have come to the apartment after Mandi was dead and opened the window. Nobody else had a key.

The men who were poking through the ruins of Betty's garage finished their business and headed for their cars. From the upstairs of Betty's house, Viola saw with mild curiosity that there'd been a fire. Something more about small-town life that she didn't care for. Spontaneous combustion in the backyard.

Viola had a fleeting moment of unease when a uniformed state trooper approached the back door and knocked. She tied the disgusting scarf she'd found in a room at Crispin's place around her head. It undoubtedly belonged to that nasty woman whose breath was heavy with alcohol. Hard to believe that attractive if despicable boy was her son. She thought he was quite taken with her. The girl had bad hair and was therefore forgettable.

Viola had, of course, enchanted Crispin. Behind his gruff exterior, he had enjoyed her company. She hated to leave him behind in the damp, smelly pool room, but business was business.

"Yes?" she said sweetly to the trooper through a crack in the back door.

"Miss Trenka? We're finished here. Officer Bob said to say he'd be coming around later."

"And most welcome he will be," Viola said. "I have some things to do now."

The trooper tipped his hat. "That front tire on your truck looks as though it could use some air, ma'am."

"Yes," Viola said. "I'll be taking it to the garage later."

"Those people in the blue car down the street—"

"Insurance," Viola said. In a manner of speaking, they were.

"About your garage, eh? Mr. Saks next door is in insurance. He'd be a good bet now that you've moved to town."

"Yes, yes," Viola said impatiently. She hated to be without makeup and have this man assume her to be the dowdy and unattractive Betty. Tina strolled out to the kitchen and observed the slightly open door. "Young man, I do have some urgent matters. My hair . . . things."

Tina decided on a morning stroll and headed rather spryly toward the open door.

"No!" Viola shrieked. "Bad, bad precious. Nasty, dirty grass." She scooped up the cat and beamed at the trooper. "She hates the country."

The trooper tipped his hat again, and departed, thinking that Bob's description of Betty Trenka was way off. She was definitely not a sensible, down-to-earth person; she was batty.

Viola went upstairs to mend the ravages of the terrible night in the pool room. The basic mascara, blush, and lipstick and the tube of wrinkle eraser in her bag would have to do. Betty, to Viola's delight, actually had a container of hair spray to fix her hairdo. And thank goodness for little black dresses in fabulous material that scarcely wrinkled.

She would have liked to shower and relax, but Betty was sure to be back soon. She was probably in town buying newspapers, and hopefully more cat food. Then there was Rosellen, who had better be there soon. She wished she had her own car, but she saw that it was gone from the road. Probably towed under some silly town ordinance about not parking on seldom-used roads. She had the pickup. It would get her to some nice car rental place. Then she was on the road to Boston. She'd have to wait awhile before she returned to New York, until the murder and things had blown over. That wouldn't happen until after the press interest died down. She wondered how much she'd make from that. . . .

She was working on her face upstairs, when she heard the door downstairs open.

Betty at last. Rosellen would have rung the bell.

"I'm up here," Viola called out cheerfully. "What a time I have had."

* * *

It was only minutes from the Winfield farm to Betty's house, but she crammed a lot of thinking into them as she drove along Timberhill Road.

Viola had blithely left Crispin Abbott locked away in the pool room without a backward glance. Betty was pretty sure that she had fled in the pickup truck—no doubt unrecognizable as the glamorous Violetta after her difficult night—and certainly had headed to Betty's place in the hope of encountering Rosellen and her blackmail money.

Once she had the money, would Viola continue to keep quiet, or would she tell the authorities who the murderer was, or at least what she thought she knew? And what she knew was, in Betty's thinking, that either Rosellen or her husband had killed Mandi Webb.

What would Viola do then?

Then Betty had it.

Sanctuary. How many times had that word been used lately? Sister Rita, Rosellen, and by Viola herself, according to Crispin.

Sanctuary meant a place beyond the reaches of the law, with religious connotations. Viola's memories of childhood teachings had stuck somewhere in her mind.

Why would Viola need sanctuary?

Because she wanted to be beyond the clutches of the law.

Viola might well be settling old scores with Rosellen, and seeking to profit at the same time, but Betty suspected that neither of the Hamiltons was guilty of murder.

Viola, however, very likely was.

She spotted the pickup parked in her driveway, she saw the photographers' dirty blue car on the shoulder a short distance down the road. And she noticed something else that alarmed her somewhat. An unfamiliar station wagon, expensive and with Connecticut plates was parked in front of the house. It was so "weekend home in Litchfield" that it had to belong to the Hamiltons.

Betty could not imagine what she would find when she entered. The least bothersome would be merely an unpleasant confrontation between the Hamiltons on one side and Viola on the other.

She pulled into the drive behind the pickup and went around to the back door. Since she was certain that Viola had murdered Mandi Webb, she could not imagine why the Hamiltons ever considered paying Viola blackmail money for a crime neither of them had committed.

She opened the back door quietly and stepped into her kitchen. She could hear voices from the living room. An angry man, an angry woman, then unmistakably Viola's voice.

"I *assumed*, darlings. Henry was so involved with the girl. Who else could it have been?"

The man said, "It could just as easily have been Rosie."

"But it wasn't, and you both know it." That was Rosellen.

"You don't get a cent from us," Henry said. "And we're going to the police about this."

"Oh, darlings, don't. I needed the money, that's all it was. For all the little things I need. I didn't see anything, I just imagined—"

"Let's go, Rosie."

Betty walked into the living room.

"Betty, thank goodness!" Viola said. "There's been a terrible misunderstanding."

Betty looked at the three of them. "There has indeed," she said. "Which one of you murdered Mandi Webb?"

"Who are you?" Henry Hamilton said.

"Betty Trenka. This is my house."

"Miss Trenka, this woman has tried to blackmail me . . . us," Rosellen said. "She made me believe that Henry had murdered that poor child."

"But I didn't," Henry said. "I admit I let myself into Viola's apartment while she was supposed to be away, but . . . but Mandi was dead." He looked pained at the memory. "I opened the window to air the place, but I couldn't bring myself to go to the police. I didn't want to become a suspect. I finally convinced Rosie that I couldn't have done it."

"And I convinced him that I didn't," Rosellen said.

"That settles that, then," Betty said. "Perhaps you'd best leave now."

"I just wanted to see her face when I turned down the idea of blackmail," Rosellen said. "I'll leave your things on the walk when we leave. Here's your portfolio."

She pulled the black leather case from her carryall and dropped it on the floor. Tina had been sitting on the arm of the sofa, but leapt to the floor and disappeared behind the sofa.

Rosellen glared one last time at Viola and marched out of the house, followed by Henry.

"Well, that didn't work out, did it?" Viola said. She looked quite downcast.

"Viola," Betty said. "Suppose you tell me what really happened."

"Nothing happened, except what I told you," Viola said. "After I found Mandi I just imagined things, I guess." She went to the window and looked out. "That damned Rosie. She had my makeup all the time. She's just left my cases out there by the road." Viola turned around and said pleadingly, "Please, please, go out and get them for me, Betty. The photographers are right down the road, waiting. I *can't* let them see me like this."

"If I do, then will you tell me the truth?"

"I have to leave for Boston soon," Viola said. "It's a long drive and I want to get there before dark."

"Sanctuary," Betty said.

There was a glimmer of something in Viola's eyes that made Betty think that she understood what Betty knew but she still wasn't going to let go.

"Something like that. I need a new life."

"Surely you don't think Rita and the sisters are going to allow you to become one of them." Betty knew now for certain that Viola's grasp of what was done and what wasn't was nonexistent.

"No. Probably not. But something will work out. Now,

please, please, bring my makeup case. There's still a chance I can profit handsomely from the interest of the media."

Betty gave up. "You can't get away with it, Viola."

"It?"

"Murder. I started putting together all the times and days you were supposed to be there and here. You killed that poor girl and called Rita right afterward. She told me you'd called several days ago when you were very upset. That's when you got my address and phone number. You went away, came back to your apartment to feed Tina. Shrimp. Two days before you came here that night. But you'd already been to East Moulton to locate me precisely, and perhaps to pass the time until you could reasonably appear at your apartment as if coming back from a week in New Jersey."

"She was hateful," Viola said. "And she was going to tell Rosie about her and Henry, and Henry would stop paying me for my silence."

"You killed her for that little?"

"I was very angry," Viola said. "These things happen."

"Stay right here while I bring in your things."

Betty thought fast while she walked to the two cases Rosellen had left on the shoulder. She would have to summon the police, of course. They could handle finding proof.

Suddenly, she felt enormously sad. She'd mourned a little when she thought Viola might be dead, but this was far worse.

She picked up the bags and slowly returned to the house.

What she discovered when she entered didn't register at once. Out of the corner of her eye she saw Viola sitting on the sofa, clasping Tina in her arms. And then she found herself looking into the startlingly blue eyes of Johnny Fender.

He had a gun in his hand.

"I want my stuff," he said. "This one"—he jerked his head in Viola's direction—"she says she doesn't know anything about it, and that could be so since she was at the farm."

"I don't know what you're talking about," Betty said. Viola was bad enough, but Johnny was lethal.

"Give me a break, lady. Just tell me where it is. It's worth a fortune, and I'm not going to leave it behind."

"You're going to be leaving Carole behind," Betty said. She was desperate to delay the inevitable. She didn't think Johnny Fender was going to leave them peacefully alive after he'd picked up his drugs.

"Too bad," he said. "Come on. I don't have time to talk. And I'll want your car keys. I had to come over the fields on foot and wait until the cops finished with the garage, and then I had to wait until those people left.

"I hid it in the kitchen," Betty said, trying to keep her voice steady. There seemed to be no way out.

"Okay, both of you. In front of me. Lady, put down that cat and move."

Viola stood, but she still held tight to Tina, who squirmed in annoyance.

"We have to, Viola," Betty said.

"I thought you liked me," Viola said. She was looking old and tired, far older than her years.

Johnny didn't deign to answer, but merely waved his gun to get them moving toward the door to the kitchen.

Then several things happened.

Tina popped out of Viola's arms and skittered in Johnny's direction, upsetting his concentration on the two women. Viola shrieked and stumbled toward Tina.

Then Johnny fired.

The noise was horrendous in Betty's small living room, and she rocked backward, praying she hadn't been hit.

Someone was pounding on the front door.

Viola was lying on the floor. Red, red blood was soaking into Betty's light carpeting.

Johnny ran toward the back door as the two photographers figured out that the front door wasn't locked, and burst in.

Tina fled to safety behind the sofa.

"An ambulance," Betty gasped. She fumbled with the

phone until the woman photographer took it from her hand and dialed.

The man knelt beside Viola.

"It looks bad," he said. "I was on the police beat for a while, and I've seen stuff like this. He didn't hit you, did he?"

"No," Betty said. Her heart was pounding. "I'm all right."

But she was seeing a part of her life seeping away.

"It's going to be all right, Viola," she whispered. She tried to think of the right prayers. Sister Rita would know the right prayers.

Viola moved her lips. "I did a terrible thing, Betty. Will God forgive me?"

"God is good," Betty said.

Viola's breathing was shallow now. "I must look terrible."

Betty held her hand. There was blood on the perfect nails.

"You look beautiful, Violetta," she said. Viola's face was gray and pinched, her mascara was smudged, but her lipstick was flawless. "The way you looked on the cover of *Vogue*." She could hear the wail of the ambulance and police sirens. She felt completely helpless at a time when someone needed her more than anyone ever had.

"What was she trying to do? Save her cat?"

"Or me," Betty said. "Let's say it was me."

Viola died on the way to the hospital. The police picked up Johnny hitchhiking on the turnpike. That part was over.

Crispin Abbott had been kind. He blamed it all on Johnny, and it seemed that Carole would be reunited with Noelle.

Ted Kelso merely said, "We'll talk, Elizabeth, when you're ready."

In the late afternoon Betty had a phone call from the town librarian.

"You were supposed to volunteer today," she said crossly. "It upset my entire schedule. I can't have this."

Betty sat on the sofa with Tina at her side and looked at the bloodstain on her carpet.

"I'm sorry," Betty said. "I couldn't make it today. We are in mourning."

JOYCE
CHRISTMAS

Available at your local bookstore.
Published by Fawcett Books.